5 Months and Counting

Written By:
Elizabeth Barnes

5 Months and Counting

Written By: Elizabeth Barnes
Cover Design and Edited By: Aaron C. Butler

ISBN: 9781967082339 (Paperback)
ISBN: 9781967082346 (eBook)
Library of Congress Control Number: 2025908912

Printed in the United States of America

BookButler Publishing Company
Upper Marlboro, MD 20774

TheBookButler.com

BookButler Publishing Company titles may be purchased in bulk for educational, business, fundraising, or sales promotional use. For information, please email: info@thebookbutler.com

Dedication

This book is dedicated to a dear friend who lives over 2,500 miles away and was diagnosed with breast cancer in late 2022. The diagnosis results were not as we had hoped, and she required chemotherapy and radiation to beat it. I struggled with how I could support her from so far away during her 5-months of treatment (hence the title, 5-Months and Counting). Queuing off something I had done previously with a friend while in college during our summer breaks, I decided to write something she could read during treatment to pass the time. Every month for 5 months, I would send her what I had written, and we would discuss it as the book is riddled with connections to her and me. This book helped me stay connected and helped her pass the 5 months until it was a memory not to be repeated. She encouraged me to put this to print, so I hope you who are reading this enjoy this "time passer." Much love to my friend.

Table of Contents

Chapter 1

Jane

Winded for some odd reason after a 10-mile run, I hurry to get ready for the day. Running track in high school and college was my passion and it has stuck with me all these years, now 35. I always run outside, not on a mindless treadmill. It helps me clear my mind for the day. Reset, if you will, putting yesterday's hardships behind me only to encounter them again today.

Children's oncology is my gig. Head RN (Chief Nursing Officer) at Children's National Hospital in Washington, DC. I never pictured myself settling in DC, but after my parents died, leaving my unmarried brother without family in the city, I thought it best for us to be close. He was by no means alone as he had oodles of friends in the city that he went to Georgetown with. He was always busy playing with his band, working, or hiking but we always reserved Sunday as our sibling time to cook and reminisce about our past.

We were fortunate growing up. My dad worked for the State Department as a Foreign Service Officer. He was first posted in Ethiopia, where he met my mother. From there, they moved to Morocco, where my brother and I were born. Went back many years later – what an amazing country. Our next post was Nicaragua where I attended a Spanish kindergarten. Hard to imagine that I spoke Spanish as a young child. Can't speak a lick now. This is where my memories of growing up really kick in, though only in bits and pieces. My brother has a much better memory than me and I am always amazed at the level of detail he remembers. Our last post was in Senegal, West Africa. I am flooded with memories of our time there, as we were there for well over six years. I still have several friends from there that I am friends with today. I find that simply amazing.

Shit! It is 7 am, and I have to be at work by 7:30 am. See how my mind clears and wanders with a run! I've got time for a quick rinse. Thank God for scrubs - no wardrobe decisions required. Work is just a short walk away, and I – Need - Coffee! I'd better order ahead. I am off and only hope my kiddos today have a better day than yesterday. I always hope.

As I step out of the shower, my phone rings. Where's my damn phone? My brother is always telling me to leave it in the same place so that I remember where it is. I never remember to do that. It's Kate – damn. I don't have time to talk to her. She goes on and on and never takes the hint that I need to go. She will be annoyed but I will just have to call her later.

Chapter 2

Kate

It never fails. Every time I call Jane, she never answers. I wonder if I should take that personally. I know she's busy and all, taking care of sick kids, but I need to speak with her urgently. I mean, hell! She isn't married (any longer). She does not have any kids of her own. Why can't she just pick up the phone? She is never going to believe my luck! She's probably already on her way to work, so best to text her to call me urgently when she gets a minute.

I hurdle upstairs to make sure the kids are getting ready for school. Hurdles. That is actually where I met Jane. We both were on scholarship at the University of Hawaii for Track and Field. She was a much better runner, but I could clear some hurdles. We were roomed together our very first year and kept it that way throughout our 4 years. Though we had Track and Field in common, we were polar opposites when it came to our field of study and our social life. I was studying to be an engineer, and Jane was pre-med. Socially I couldn't give a damn about where the next party was, but Jane was always plugged in. Regardless, we both relied on our scholarships for completely different reasons to finish, so at the end of the day, we were both focused.

As I mount the last stair, I pause and take a moment to roll my eyes. My daughter, Carly, just shy of 11, is talking on her phone in front of her mirror while applying make-up that she should not be wearing, and my son, Jackson, age 6, is listening to Glenn Gould play Bach's Goldberg Variations for the millionth time with his EarPods in. Was I this challenging as a child? Note to self – check in with dad to make sure he got his prescription filled. Like synchronized swimmers, Carly and Jackson look my way and mimic my eye roll as they mutter, "Coming!" I hurry back downstairs as my cell phone begins to ring. Good – Kate is finally calling me back. Wrong. Damn. It was my dad. I will call him from the car as I take the kids to school.

As we pile into my used but fabulous Porsche, my phone rings again. It's my husband, Tom, of 12 years, reminding me to take Jackson's inhaler to school. I am the most organized person on the planet. I don't need reminding of something that is life or death for my son. I breathe and answer politely, "Got it!" About five minutes into the 35-minute ride, I call my dad. Meds refilled. Check. Now, I can enjoy the California coastal highway traffic which is backed up with a sea of red lights for miles. Great. Kids are going to be late to school again.

My phone rings the distinctive duck quack, which lets me know it's Jane. I answer with excitement, "Jane! Finally! You will never believe my luck!" She answers calmly, "Well, hi, Kate. I am about to walk into the hospital. I have 5 minutes. What's up?" "Jane," I say again, taking a very deep breath, "I inherited a boatload of money! We're talking millions, and the very first thing I want to do is take a girls' trip! I am thinking of Hawaii! We can surprise visit our beloved track coach, Ginny! Then, we can fly to Nags Head and Virginia Beach to spend some time with Jules and Justin (the twins who ran track with us). The possibilities are endless!" "Kate. Kate. Slow down, my friend, before you have a heart attack. Where is this all coming from?" asks Jane. I know what Jane is thinking. I came from nothing. My scholarship was the only thing allowing me to go to college. "I know it is a lot to digest. Look, I am in the car with the kids. Can we talk after your shift, and I will explain everything?" I respond. "Sure, sure," Jane says. "Great, I will text you to connect later today. Love you. Bye." I am giddy with excitement, but I can't get ahead of myself. Jane and I will have to figure out our work coverage as I plan on being away for, say, four months. I know I can convince her to do it. I will appeal to her adventurous side. That's it! One month to plan and four months to travel. Geez, will this traffic ever move? I will need a well laid out plan with full coverage for the kids if Tom is going to buy into it. Maybe I will surprise him with a week-long surf trip with his buddies from out East. Yeah, that ought to do it. Before I end my thought, I am in front of the kids' school, and they are slamming the doors, muttering goodbye. I guess my autopilot is in full gear. I really need to be more careful when driving. That is a mental note I will probably never recall.

Chapter 3

Tom

I can hear the sarcasm in Kate's voice when I call her to remind her about the inhaler. It is a big win for me when I remind her of something she has forgotten. To be honest, it rarely happens. Jackson had a pretty bad asthma attack over the weekend, we think due to exposure to pet dander. One of the reasons we moved to California was to escape his triggers caused by pollen and bad weather, but it's hard to avoid pets, especially when they reside at newly formed friends' houses. We forgot to ask if they had any pets! That one is on me, as I did drop off. Kate was good about not blaming me. We are past the blame game on this one. We just haven't found a pulmonologist who can address Jackson's allergies so that his attacks remain at bay. It might be a good idea to go back out East to Children's, as Jane has suggested many times, to get another opinion. I am sure Kate would love to spend a few days with Jane in DC. Hell, what am I saying? I would love to go back out East to visit my once hometown and old friends, and maybe even get in a little East Coast surfing in. I don't get to go back much now that all of my family resides out West, but I have great memories from our time there. Virginia Beach, Virginia, is never a town that I would write off and not visit. I drool slightly at the thought of wings from Big Sam's, a local restaurant in Virginia Beach that I frequented. I have never been able to find another place that could top their double grilled wings.

My mind shifts to recent headlines reporting that my company's stock is sinking as the market gains. Lockheed Martin (LMT) is lagging, and I am taxed with solutioning in this fucked up market. The Zacks Industry Rank, which gauges the strength of our industry groups (ours being the Aerospace sector), currently has our industry ranked at 87, which puts us in the top 35% of our 250+ industry. Based on this ranking, we should be outperforming by a factor of 2 to 1, but we aren't. Kate took her engineering degree a different route and has become quite a technical expert in her field, working for WSP USA. I am really proud of what she has accomplished, considering her meager beginnings. But now, somehow, she has become the sole inheritor of her mother's uncle's fortune, who we didn't even know existed. Kate came from nothing, and I mean nothing, so how she had an uncle with a fortune is a mystery to us and will remain a mystery as her mother is deceased, and the inheritance came upon her uncle's death. Who knows if we will really ever know the full story. Kate's father seems to be in the dark as well.

All of Kate's professionalism has gone out the window with this news. She is like a kid visiting a candy store for the very first time. I get it but this isn't a rag to riches story as she has experienced success and financial wealth on her own. Let's hope Jane can reel her in from her elation over this financial windfall. I've tried, but she is still on an emotional roller coaster, and the ride never seems to end. My practical Kate appears to be imploding, but I suspect it won't be long before she has a plan. A practical plan.

Chapter 4

Jane

have never once heard Kate hysterical or giddy. She was always the serious one, so this felt unsettling. Maybe I will try to ring her again during one of my breaks rather than wait until my shift ends. That will be surprising to her, I am sure. She is always so good about calling. Keeping in touch. It is not that I don't think of her or wonder what she is up to. I guess I just suck as a friend. Other than work, running the occasional 25K, and time with my brother, I don't have much else occupying my time. I could make more of an effort.

I did marry my college boyfriend, Mark, right after college, but in our first year of marriage, he tragically died while crossing the street on his way to work. Apparently, a motorcycle came out of nowhere and hit him, knocking him off his feet. I was told he got up and appeared to be okay but then collapsed, as he had suffered severe head trauma, which caused an acute subdural hematoma. There was nothing they could do; I was told over and over again. I was not nearby as I was in nursing school about an hour away and, of course, had my phone turned off during class. Nothing seemed real until I saw him lying there, lifeless. We hadn't started a family as I wanted to get through nursing school first. Oddly, when I do go out on an occasional date now, my mind always drifts back to Mark and the judgment and comparison kicks in. That usually ruins the moment and date unless there is alcohol involved, which might result in a one-night stand that I immediately regret. It has been 13 years since Mark passed. I made a mental note to check in with Connie, one of our clinical psychologists at the hospital. She probably has some words of wisdom for me, hopefully not riddled with sarcasm as her comments usually are. God, I love that.

Today, little Marcus, one of my long-time patients, is due to go home on hospice. He has recently undergone his 3rd operation to remove tumored tissue, which did not go well. Surgeons had to exit the surgery without removing all as the cancer had overtaken his little body. He is going to die, and there was nothing I could do about it. As I enter his room to do his final check before discharge, he greets me with a grin I will soon not forget. He informs me that his g-tube had buggies in it, so I immediately check his abdomen. Marcus has the presence of infection causing excessive tension between the internal and external bolster. The infection is rampant due to organ rejection, so the only course of action is antibiotics, which are not taking effect, and pain medication, which he will be released with. I look at his mom, and we nod in understanding. This little tike has been through so much. My goal with him is to keep him pain-free and happy for as long as time will allow. I don't expect more than two weeks maximum for Marcus to be with us. He will be discharged and return to Hampton, Virginia, to be with his family. It will be hard to let him go.

Just as I pat him on the head, my beeper goes off. Kirsten, an eight-month-old baby who has recently arrived, has neuroblastoma, stage 4. She is a precious little thing and her parents are so young. Neuroblastoma is an ugly cancer, but we have gotten past it in many instances, and I will be damned if I let this little one succumb to it. Kirsten needs my immediate attention, so I say my goodbyes and give a high five to Marcus, give the in-room nurse some final instructions, and then move on to attend to Kirsten. Before exiting the room, I look back one more time at Marcus, who flashes a grin at me. I will hold his smile in my heart forever.

Kirsten is the last on my morning rounds, so I take the opportunity to try and connect with Kate. Millions of dollars. I have to know where this is coming from. Kate had never spoken of any rich relative or the opportunity for an inheritance. I try her cell phone but she does not pick up. Maybe I should call Tom to get his take? He is sometimes easier to talk to. Tom also does not pick up, but I suspect he is dealing with LHM's current headlines, which I heard about on my walk to the hospital. As I am about to head back out to continue rounds, my phone rings. Kate.

"Kate," I say, "Fill me in!"

Chapter 5

Kate

I can hear the intrigue in Jane's voice. I knew it would be easy to hook her in on my plans. I slowly and calmly explain to Jane the circumstances that landed me this fortune. What I now know is that my mother had an uncle that lived in Europe. France, to be exact. I have never met him, and as far as I know, my mother had never visited him. She did speak German, oddly enough, but not French. I am not sure why we never got behind the story of why she spoke German. Apparently, this uncle was one of the richest men in Europe, with a net worth of $148 billion. Yup, I said billion! To think of it, he is not far behind Elon Musk, whose net worth is somewhere in the $200 billions. Anyway, his name is Francois Dubois, and he is famously known in the fashion and cosmetic industry. The name meant nothing to me or Will when I received notice of his death, but Jane explodes with excitement when I mention his name.

"Kate, you had never heard of him?" asks Jane. Of course, Jane recognizes the name as she wears nothing but high fashion. Maybe it is because she has to compensate for wearing scrubs most of the time. I never understood spending that kind of money on clothes and shoes. Well maybe now I will splurge on a few items! "Jane," I respond, "of course, I have no idea who he is or even that my mother had a living uncle!" I continue by informing her that shortly following his death, I received a call from his Executor, Delphine Renault, who informed me that aside from his many charities and causes, he has willed me a small fortune. "Jane, I am talking of $500 million dollars. Can you believe it? Apparently, he never married and has no children and I am the only living relative! Tom is still in disbelief and is doing research to make sure this isn't a mistake that comes back to bite us, but Kate, I already have the money!" I am rambling and I can hear Jane trying to interrupt. I pause and listen to the line of questions that ensues.

"Kate, first, congratulations! You've always played the lottery as if a win was going to happen, and voila! A bigger payout than you could have ever imagined. Second, what the hell, Kate? Is this really real? Did you do an Ancestry.com on this guy? Your mom never mentioned him? What's Tom saying about this?" says Jane. I continue to share with Jane as much information as I have until her questions begin to subside. There is no reasonable explanation but yeah, I should definitely do an Ancestory.com on him. Why didn't I think of that? "Look, Jane, it is real. I have the money. Now we have to figure out how to spend some of it, and of course, I immediately thought of you. We have been busting our asses since high school, so it is time for us to take a break, enjoy the fortune bestowed upon me, and..."

I can hear Jane's beeper going off. That means a kiddo needs her immediate attention. "Kate, listen, I have to go. You know the drill. I am just thrilled for you and would love to discuss this more. I have a few days off coming up. Why don't I fly out your way so we can sit down and talk this through?" says Jane. "Yes!" I respond. "That is exactly what I was hoping you would say. Send me the details when you have them." We say our goodbyes, and both get back to work – the back of our minds reeling with ideas of what's to come.

Chapter 6

Ginny

Coaching is wearing on me after 40 years, and I know Gerald is getting tired of waiting on me to explore this beautiful island we live on. I have given the University of Hawaii notice that I needed to retire by year-end, but they are dragging their feet, and they will soon be stuck without a track and field coach because I promised Gerald this was it.

It hasn't been the same since our boys graduated from U of H, but every year, I get kids that I have to see through. I tend to mother hen my team, especially the ones here on scholarship. I know this has got to end. I am reminded of that by Gerald almost on a daily basis. He has his activities and loves, but he does not want to do the big exploring until I can go with him.

Before my battered knees can't handle it anymore, Gerald wants to go on one of the many expert-level hikes in Oahu. The one that has caught his eye is the Moanalua Middle Ridge trail, which is only about a 12-mile round trip hike but involves some rope climbing and scrambling up barely-there dirt trails. Though I cannot run anymore, I do think I can tackle this challenge. I have read that once you reach the summit, you are greeted with views of Kane'ohe, Kailua, and Mokoli'I that are breathtaking. I am sure the boys can't join us, as they are living their lives in different states, but it sure would be nice to have them along. Best to just keep this between Gerald and me. He would appreciate that.

Coach Davidson, our strength and conditioning coach, steps into my office to let me know that our Program Director, Coach Parker, would like to see me. Good. Maybe they have a plan. I have this odd sense of sadness and relief as I walk across the field to get to the main building. Coaching has been such a big part of my life that it will be hard to let it go. On the other hand, my boys have now had kids, and I don't want to miss too much of their growing up, so I need to be able to leave at the drop of a hat. Bittersweet, as the saying goes. Coach Parker waves me into his office.

"Aloha Ginny! Great practice today. Lizzie really flies like a gazelle over the pole vault, no? She was a good find." I can tell he is a bit nervous. I decide to torture him a bit, as the team often does, because he is just so gullible. "She is fantastic, John, a real charger. She is making me reconsider my retirement," I say, "I mean, how can I even contemplate leaving with our current roster of 10 out of 23 on scholarship? That is our biggest number yet. You know how I am, John." John shuffles some papers on his desk and looks up from underneath his glasses, slightly bewildered. His eyes seem to question my statement. I keep my look of excitement steady. "Ginny, you can't be serious? You gave me a hard deadline to find your replacement. I feel as if I have been unfair to you in dragging it out this long. What are you saying?" says John. "John, relax. Just having a bit of last-minute fun at your expense. So, who's it gonna be? Last time we chatted, you were down to three potential candidates. All excellent, in my opinion. Have you shortlisted the shortlist? Tell me I can go home today and put Gerald out of his misery."

John knows my preference is Andrea Simkins from the College of William and Mary. She has experience at all levels, is a certified strength and conditioning specialist, and has coached several elite athletes both domestically and internationally. In addition, she has a strong history of advocating for athletes requiring scholarships. I would feel settled leaving, as U of H would be in good hands. "Ginny, yes, yes. We have made up our minds, and I think you will be pleased to know we have decided to go with your recommendation, Andrea Simkins. She is willing to relocate immediately so she can be up and running for the Spring training with a bit of tutelage from you," John sighs. "Now Ginny, I know what you are going to say, but it is just one more month! Surely Gerald would understand..."

"John, relax. That will be fine. Gerald will completely understand, and we need the time to plan some activities that we want to do. I am happy to stay on board to show Andrea the ropes, but let's let her take the lead. She will be fine. I will slowly wean my hours as the weeks progress, which will surely give Gerald a sense that the end is near. Deal?" I say. "Deal, Ginny! I can't thank you enough. I will let you know her arrival date soon, and then we can plan as a team how this will all work out. Let's not forget that we are planning a strong send-off for you, so that will really make it official for Gerald!" says John. "Oh boy, okay. I'll allow it," I say with a smirk. I am not big on celebrating me, but I know the team will want to do something and I can't deprive them of that. I exit John's office feeling a bit anxious because this is all I have known and done for the last 40 years. Will I be satisfied not working and coaching? Maybe I can find a part-time coaching gig at one of the High Schools. Jesus. I tell myself to give it a rest as I head back to my office to share with Gerald the good news.

Chapter 7

Jane

My trip out West was a whirlwind in more ways than one. I hardly had a moment of rest with Kate bouncing off the walls. Deservedly so. Inheriting such a large sum of money would be exciting to anyone, but for someone like Kate, whose rough upbringing left her to fend for herself, it's beyond anything imaginable.

Of course, after endless amounts of DuckDuckGo searches, we were well versed on the uncle, though Ancestry.com did not reveal the connection between Kate's mom and uncle. We decided to add Paris as a leg to our adventure to see if we could uncover anything. Who doesn't want to go to Paris?

We were able to lay out our destination plan with the help of one of my friends, Sasha, who just happens to be a Travel Advisor. We would use the month of January to plan and then travel for four months. There was no issue getting Tom on board with the plan because Kate had thought of everything. He was genuinely excited for her, and the kids - well, let's just say they were not disappointed with what Kate had in store for them. Each with their own mini adventure on her relatives' dime.

I am, however, worried about Jackson. His asthma is not under control, so I convince Kate to take Jackson out East before we leave for a full workup with our Allergist and Immunologist at Children's. I decide not to warn her about Dr. Shad's bedside manner, as it is quite gruff and matter-of-fact. I'll handle the interpretation.

Tom convinced us to fly privately vs. trying to stick to scheduled flights. Kate's sarcastic but mischievous response was, "Why not? I can afford it!" So weird to hear those words coming out of her mouth. Makes sense. This would lend us the flexibility to change our path if desired. The cost would barely make a dent in the inheritance, after all, so I mimicked, "Why not!" I took the lead on jotting everything down as I would have to relay it to Sasha:

<u>The "Plan"</u>
1. California to Hawaii (Oahu)
2. Hawaii to Norfolk
3. Norfolk to Paris
4. Paris to Greece
5. Greece to Egypt
6. Egypt to Morocco
7. Morocco to South Africa
8. South Africa to Australia
9. Australia to California

Kate was gracious enough to agree to visit the countries that I grew up in, plus a few that we both dreamed of going to. She never had the opportunity to travel, so it was a win-win for both of us.

When I arrive home, my mind is in a tailspin. I will have to get things covered at work and give my brother all the necessary paperwork in case I decide to cliff jump or something and don't make it back. That makes me chuckle as I recall the last time I cliff-jumped in Jamaica. What was I thinking? Ah, to be young and unafraid. Kate, of course, wouldn't do the jump, but maybe this time I can convince her. This is her adventure, and I will make sure it is a memorable one.

I unpack, grab my iPad, and head upstairs to get some sleep. I don't think I was out West long enough to get jet lag. As I settle in to watch a little British drama, my phone dings. It's a text from Marcus's mother. My heart sinks. I open the text and read:

> *"Jane, I thought you would want to know. Marcus is now with Jesus in Heaven. He had a few good days here at home, but he took a turn yesterday and passed early this morning. The hospice folks from Edmarc, who you referred us to, were so nice and took such good care of him. I just didn't think this would happen so quickly. We just weren't ready. We did everything we could, right? I keep questioning myself. Anyway, again sorry to text so late. I just wanted to say thank you for everything. He loved his time with you."*
>
> *– Dorothy.*

One is never prepared for these moments. Flashes of images of Marcus roll through my mind. Life without him on earth is incomprehensible. He was such a light, even through all the pain. I think that is what drew me to pediatric oncology. These kids are superhumans. They make me want to be a better person. I learn so much more from the little ones than I do from adults, it seems. It is a puzzling thought. I must respond to Dorothy.

> *"Dorothy, thanks so much for letting me know. I am heartbroken. Marcus was such a light. Yes, we did do everything we possibly could and then some. We ran out of options. Let's speak in the next couple of days and please send me the details of his funeral. I want to try and come if I can swing it. I am so sorry, Dorothy. He was one of a kind."*

I meant it. Though there are many kids just as sweet as Marcus, Marcus was wise beyond his years, caring more about his family than himself. Selflessness. That is what Marcus taught me. British comedy will have to wait. My eyes are heavy from the news, so I turn off my light, snuggle in tight, and drift off with only thoughts of Marcus.

Chapter 8

Kate

The thought of Tom managing Jackson's new diagnosis and protocol without me to keep his asthma under control seemed daunting. Somehow, within a few weeks, Jane was able to get Jackson in at Children's with Dr. Shad, a world-renowned Allergist and Immunologist. If Jane hadn't been present, I would have walked out, leaving Dr. Shad in mid-rant. He was appalled that Jackson had been treated as if he was allergic to certain allergens when, in fact, that wasn't the case at all. A simple blood test revealed that Jackson had Eosinophilic asthma (e-asthma), which apparently is driven by too many eosinophils, a type of white blood cell in the body. The heart-wrenching part of the diagnosis was that the rescue inhalers and oral steroids he was taking were exacerbating the issue. Dr. Shad put Jackson on Fasenra, which will allow us to begin to reduce Jackson's dependency on oral steroids. Tom would have to manage the wean and frequent bloodwork required to get the Fasenra prescription right. We decided to hire a caregiver to support Tom during the transition. Jane thought this was completely overkill, but I wouldn't be able to relax and enjoy our adventure without Tom having extra support. I also hired a cook/housekeeper to keep the house in order and to keep an eye on the kids when they got home from school. Plus, I decided to get the kids a puppy (the cutest little West Highland Terrier we named Finley) once we learned that Jackson was NOT allergic to dogs. They were not too pleased about the dotty Doubtfire look alike, but after 2-3 Finley potty accidents in the house, the kids were grossed out enough to welcome help.

Everything seems to be falling into place. Kate was able to schedule coverage, and I simply let them know I was going on a "sabbatical" of sorts. Engineering consulting firms have been chomping at the bit to support WSP USA in 2023. Once I let the firm know I was forgoing my salary during the 4-month period, they bent to my will. To further establish good faith, I managed the RFP and incoming proposals to select the consultant needed to cover. There was nothing they could do but wave a bientot ("see you soon" in French) when I exited the office. Sadly, I did not achieve my goal of learning a bit of French during our one month of planning, but I loaded the Duolingo app so Jane and I can at least learn how to ask for directions in Paris.

It is around 8 pm on the East Coast, so I decide to call Jane to check in on our final plans. Her friend, Sasha, has done an excellent job securing us a chartered jet, which will be available to us for the full four months. All of our stay arrangements are finalized as well, which I left up to Jane and Sasha as I did not have a clue where we should stay. Remarkably, Jane answers on the first ring, "Kate, hey, I was just getting ready to call you. Any questions about the final itinerary? Are there any changes you want to make?" As if! The whole trip seems like a dream to me. I am ready to get started. "Jane, everything looks perfect," I reply. "Sunday's the big day! Were you able to reach Coach Ginny?" "Nope, I called her cell and sent her an email. She is probably wrapped up in the season. She will love that we just dropped in and surprised her. I can't wait to see her face when we walk up to the track during practice. To think it has been 9 years since either of us have been back. Look, Kate, I just wanted to say thank you for bringing me along on this journey. We are going to make some unforgettable memories, and there is no one I would rather do this with. Truly," Jane responds. "Jane," I reply, feeling the love for my dear friend, "There is no one else I would do this with. Period. Holy shit, I cannot believe we are finally leaving on Sunday! I will pick you up from the airport tomorrow. Text me when you board so that I know your flight is on time." We squeal our good-byes in unison and hang up. As I pull up the driveway, Finley's adorable white head is peering out the window, and he starts to bark in excitement. Jackson soon appears and waves madly as he scoops up Finley to give him a hug. Finley has stolen our hearts already.

Chapter 9

Jane

Leg 1 - Hawaii

We board our private jet, which is huge for just the two of us. The seats apparently convert into beds. It is staffed with two male stewards (good one, Sasha) who will be with us for the entire trip. Kate was practically hyperventilating while saying goodbye to her family for four months. I couldn't be more excited to visit the places I have not been to in a very long time. I can't wait to share with Kate everything from my childhood, though I am sure so much has changed. My brother is green with envy, but he knows this is a chance of a lifetime that I cannot pass up. He mentioned briefly that he may be joining us, maybe mid-way through, in either Egypt or Morocco. Kate cheered at the thought, so he put the wheels in motion, understanding that our plans were not completely scheduled. Nevertheless, I will keep him informed as we progress.

It will take us about six hours to get to our destination in Hawaii, so Kate and I settle in, and I ask the very handsome steward to open a bottle of champagne. To our surprise, champagne had already been sitting on ice, courtesy of Kate's husband. What a doll. Kate is one lucky gal to have Tom. One of the stewards, who I now know is named Dylan, pours us each a glass. Did he just wink at me? Geez, he's hot. It's been a while since I have flirt-ed, and Dylan is clearly several years younger than me. Without breaking eye contact, Dylan asks if there is any-thing else we need before they prepare for takeoff. Okay, I am not imagining this. I mutter quickly, "Thanks, Dylan; I think we are good and ready." Jesus, that sounded stupid. He chuckles and then begins to prepare the cabin with steward #2, which, for the life of me, I have already for-gotten his name. Kate clues in and begins to nudge me the "go get yourself some girl" nudge. Then she bursts out in laughter and begins to talk a mile a minute about our time in college. Thankful for the distraction, I nestle into the seat and listen to Kate intently.

"Jane, as soon as we settle in at the hotel, let's head straight over to the campus. I want to catch Ginny before she leaves for the day. We could always surprise her at her house, but I really want to set my eyes on the school again and see some of the other staff. What do you think?" asks Kate. "Perfect plan, my friend. I am at your disposal," I respond. Kate continues to reminisce as I try to catch Dylan's eye. He hasn't once looked my way again. I must have imagined the wink. I turn to face Kate so I can be fully in the moment for her. Let the adventures begin. One month of planning down. Four months of adventure to go.

Chapter 10

Kate

Oh, I saw it. That wink. Their eye-lock. Nothing wrong with a little romance on our trip - for Jane, of course. There has been little to no romance in Jane's life since Mark passed, and it is high time. Mark was one of a kind – handsome, athletic, adventurous, intelligent. He checked off all the boxes, and once Jane met him, there was no one else for her. Since Mark died, she has dated from time to time, but they just never measured up. I've got to dig into that now that I have Jane all to myself for the next four months. She was happier when she had Mark. She is ever so serious now, which I am sure her job also attributes to. I need to get her plugged back in like she was in college. There is no room for two serious people on this trip!

Jane leans over to me and whispers, "It's time we give Dylan a nickname." Oh, here we go. This was our trademark in college: to give nicknames to people so we could talk freely without anyone really knowing who we were talking about. "I say GG for Greek God. He is definitely how I would imagine a Greek God," I say. Jane nods in agreement, and we burst out laughing, which makes GG finally look over at us. Oh, this is gonna be fun.

We chat endlessly as if no time has passed. Jane fills me in on Marcus's end with emotion as though he was her own. How she does this day in and day out is beyond me. I can barely handle Jackson's issues, and when he is really struggling, I shut down. Even though Jane sees pain and suffering on a daily basis, she doesn't seem to be bothered by it. Her approach is palliative, providing relief from the symptoms and stress of the illness, not just for the child but for the whole family - while she works with the medical team to find the right medical solutions. She goes above and beyond helping the families navigate the waters of chronic conditions, which allows the families to focus on their child in the present. As I look at her, I can see how this path she chose has worn on her a bit, but she is a beauty through and through, and her smile must bring a lot of comfort to the families. I'm just so proud of her.

The pilot comes out of the cockpit to let us know that we will be landing in 30 minutes. Geez, has it been over 6 hours already? We look at each other with excitement as we hurry to straighten up our stuff, take a bathroom break, and buckle in. We both take a moment to peer out of our windows to take in the beauty below us. My God, how I have missed this place. I will never get over the lushness of the island and the color of the water. We spent so much time exploring the island during our four years at University, it felt like home. Holy crap, Ginny is going to have a cow when she sees us! I hope Ginny and Gerald are ready for a little fun, and they will have to cancel whatever plans they have for the next few days. We have a lot of catching up to do, and I want to check out all the changes made at the University of Hawaii since we have been gone. That and have one (or more) of Ginny's famous martinis at her new place, which I heard was pretty fantastic. I yell, "Ginny's martinis," as I look away from the window at Jane. She responds with an immediate "hell yes!"

Stepping out of the plane onto the tarmac feels surreal. Was this all really happening? How was this happening? I am bound and determined to learn more about my mom's uncle in Paris. Our private car is waiting to whisk us off to the hotel to freshen up before heading over to the campus. Practice should have just started, so we will probably get there just as it is wrapping up. Perfect! In unison, Jane and I turn and wave to "the boys" and attempt to strut our stuff to the car. They smile and wave back, but not before I catch Jane in eye-lock, once again, with GG. Oh yes, this is gonna happen.

Chapter 11

Jane

We chat away as we are driven to campus, wondering what Ginny's reaction will be. She hasn't seen us in several years, but time has been kind to us both. Ginny, I am sure, is as vibrant as ever with her platinum blond hair and sleek physique. Though her knees don't allow her to run anymore, she works out every day, managing to keep herself fit despite menopause, which often wreaks havoc on women. Thankfully, both Kate and I did not sustain any injuries while running track, so we both still enjoy frequent runs – me a little more as I have more time on my hands.

The campus is as beautiful as ever, with lush green mountains surrounding it. As soon as we see the Rec center, both Kate and I lean forward to catch a glimpse of the athletics complex. Sure enough, practice is still in progress and the girls are in their green uniforms. Kate instructs the driver where to let us off, and just like that, we are standing in front of the outdoor track field, scanning the field for a head of blonde hair.

"Do you see her? I'm not seeing her. Wait there's Coach Davidson and Coach Parker talking to some woman. What's Coach Parker doing on the field?" asks Kate. "I'm not seeing her either. Maybe she is doing a one-on-one with one of the girls. Let's walk over to the stand so we can see a bit better while we wait for their practice to end. It shouldn't be much longer," I reply. As we take a seat, I see Coach Parker look our way, look away, then look our way again. He has a quick discussion with Coach Davidson and then starts to walk towards us. Immediately, I feel as if I am back in college, shying at the sight of him. He is a large and stern-looking man, but he really is a big teddy bear. Ginny loves to tease him and he always falls into her trap. How fortunate we were to have such a great coaching staff that all respected each other but knew how to have fun despite how intense training was. Kate grabs my hand, as she so often did in Coach Parker's presence, and we wave.

"Kate? Jane? I can't believe it. You are back," he says. We run down the stand to greet him with a big hug. He chuckles in delight, then steps back to take a good look at us. "No one told me you were coming. To what do we owe the pleasure of your visit?"

"Coach! So great to see you.   We came to surprise Coach Ginny and whisk her off with us for a little fun. Long story, but we are on a 4-month adventure trek, and we wanted to start it with spending time with our beloved Coach. Where is she, by the way? I am not seeing her on the field. No doubt she is off somewhere doing a one-on-one with some poor soul," says Kate as she looks at me and winks. Kate and I laugh as we remember some brutal one-on-ones that we had with Coach Ginny. They were all deserved, but it usually meant we screwed up and let Coach Ginny down, which was the last thing we wanted to do. Coach Parker's smile turns to a look of confusion as he listens to Kate. "Ladies, have you not spoken to Ginny? Better yet, do you not keep up with the school news? Ginny retired last month, but before she went, she hand-picked Coach Simkins, who you can see over there with Coach Davidson," he says. We stare at the Coach and then at the field in bewilderment. How did we not know this? It has been some time since we have spoken to Coach Ginny, but not in a million years did we think she would retire. Coach Davidson walks up as we are processing the information and relays to us her final days at the University. He confirms that she still lives in the same house but may not be there as she and her husband were planning on doing some hiking shortly after her retirement. We thank the coaches, give them a big hug, and decide to wander the campus a bit before calling the car to discuss what's next.

"Let's try ringing her. I still don't believe it, but honestly, good for her. Hard to imagine her not coaching, but there you have it," I say. Kate shakes her head in disbelief as she rings Ginny's cell. It went straight to voicemail. "Let's just head over to her house. Not the surprise we were hoping for but it will still be a surprise. I will call our driver," says Kate.

Ginny's house is a short distance from the University. She spent so much time at the University that it made sense to be close. The new house is beautiful, nestled in a small private community. Ginny has our University flag flying out front, which makes me smile. Kate is the first to the door, rings the doorbell, and then begins to knock repeatedly. I grab her hand and give her a "calm down" look, and she steps back. After several attempts and no answer, we walk around to see if she is out by the pool. As we begin to round the corner, her neighbor pops out and greets us. "Hi, ladies. If you are looking for Ginny and Gerald, they aren't there. They left a few weeks ago to hike Moanalua Middle Ridge and do some camping. Honestly, I expected them home two days ago, but they haven't shown up yet. More than likely, Gerald has convinced Ginny to stay longer, but I know Ginny has a doctor's appointment scheduled for tomorrow that she did not want to miss. You know how hard it is to get doctors' appointments these days."

That might explain why Ginny's cell went straight to voicemail. We had hiked the ridge many times and were familiar with how isolated it was. It is odd that they did not return back, as planned, especially since Ginny has a doctor's appointment. We explain to Ginny's neighbor who we are, our hope to surprise her, and our travel plans. She is elated with the notion and when asked, provides us with her doctor's name so that we could call to see if Ginny checked in with their office. "I am sure there is nothing to worry about, and I am sure they will be pulling in any minute. Will you be around for a few days? Ginny will be devastated if she misses you two," says Ginny's neighbor. "We are in no rush," I respond, "and we will definitely stick around to make sure we get to spend time with Ginny before we head off on our travels." Kate writes down our numbers, and we take Ginny's neighbors, just in case one of us learns something before the other. A tinge of concern comes over me as I look one more time at Ginny's house before we head back to the car. We will ring the doctor's office while heading back to the hotel to see what we can find out. Kate is way ahead of me, already ringing the doctor's office. The office confirms that Ginny's appointment is still on the books, though she has not responded to any of their appointment confirmation notices. Definitely out of character for Ginny, but we chalk it up to Ginny and Gerald being lost in their retirement freedom. We are certain that we will hear from Ginny tonight, and we can catch up with her after her appointment.

We arrive at the beautiful Four Seasons Hotel, realizing that we are starving. After a brief conversation with the concierge, we decide on lunch and cocktails at the cabanas around the Ohana Pool. It is time for a little downtime and chat time between two besties on an adventure. Little did I know Kate had made arrangements for the stewards to stay at our hotel. As we approach our cabana, I glance towards the pool and there is GG, sprawled out on a lounger. Clearly, he had just gone for a swim as his skin was glistening in the sun. Greek God indeed. My eyes dart at Kate in reprimand, but then I smile as she rubs her hands together in excitement. I can see Kate is going to make this a thing on this trip. Hell, I should just give in to it.

Connie, the clinical psychologist at my hospital with whom I had had a few sessions before our departure, made me realize that I am wallowing in my past and haven't taken the time to get to know men beyond a brief date or dalliance. When one has loved deeply as I have, one will mourn deeply, and that often lasts much longer than other people tell us it should. I have transformed my grief into compassionate action in the world, helping others but not myself. Though strange coming from her, she convinced me to integrate meditation and yoga into my life, which I have got to say has transfigured me in a way that I never expected. In our last session before I left for California, I vowed to take care of myself and open up to relationships. Though overwhelming, it is time, and I am ready. Though I am pretty sure GG is not what Connie meant by someone I should explore this new path with, I am sure she would approve all the same. After all, she didn't say to NOT have dalliances WHILE exploring this new path!

Chapter 12

Kate

Jane looks amazing in her bikini. Her body hasn't been hit by baby-making factors as mine has. Despite I still think I look pretty damn good after having two, albeit quite a while back. I wave like a schoolgirl at GG and the other steward (steward # 2 for now), beckoning them over, much to Jane's surprise. They join us briefly, wanting to respect our space and time together. They accept my very forward request to join us at the Waterman Bar for drinks at 7 pm and then dinner at the Noe Restaurant. I had already made reservations for four. Jane just sat back and let me do all the talking. Yeah, that's right. I am in charge of making this happen. I notice, however, that steward #2 keeps trying to make eye contact, so I will have to make this perfectly clear. This is all about Jane and I am not interested in any shenanigans on this trip. Flirting, maybe, but that is where I would have to draw the line.

Following lunch and after several Tropical Moments cocktails and dips in the pool, Jane and I are sun-kissed and happy. Jane could tell that I was on a mission to find her "love" on this trip, so she shares with me her time with her psychologist. One can never know how death impacts someone. I always thought she was just too busy to have time to build relationships. She made it clear that she was ready and open, and she appreciates that I am in this with her. She notes that though GG is more than likely not "the one," she will remain open and have fun all the same. Just as she finishes off her sentence, a red cardinal comes to rest on the lounger opposite Jane. She gasps, then smiles and says, "Whelp, there is my mom weighing in. Clearly, from the birds' strong stare, that's my message to get on with it." I reach for Jane's hand and give her a squeeze. She was so close to her parents. I still see that moments like this made her miss them very much.

"I am going to fall asleep if we sit here any longer, and I want to explore the hotel grounds a bit before we head back to our rooms to get ready for dinner. There are a few boutiques close by. Let's check those out, grab an espresso shot, then head up. Good?" I ask. "Works for me," replies Jane. As we sit up, the bird flies away and Jane watches it, giving it a gentle wave goodbye.

The boutiques are posh, which is right up Jane's alley, and she is bound and determined to make sure I buy something. I try on a few Stella McCartney dresses, which are absolutely beautiful. I decide to purchase a lime green fringed double satin dress, which Jane pairs with some mid-top trainers and a crystal mesh mini tote bag. Jane chooses a silk asymmetric shirt dress in aqua blue, which matches her eyes. She pairs it with a peep toe wedge espadrille. With an endless budget, shopping sure is a lot more fun. Jane is tickled that I stepped out of the box, and I am frankly surprised at how damn good I look. Shopping is going to be a must wherever we go, especially in Paris.

We get back to our rooms, which are adjoined, to a bottle of champagne on ice waiting for us. This time, it's from Jane's brother, Jonathan, with a note:

> *Ladies – I take it you have landed safely and have successfully surprised Coach Ginny. I am sure you are several cocktails in but cheers to you both on this big adventure. I have decided to meet up with you in Egypt, since we have already been to Morocco more than once. Keep me posted so I can book. Happy travels. Be safe. See you soon.*
>
> *-XXOO Jonathan*
>
> *P.S. I am still jealous as hell.*

Jane is so lucky to have such a great sibling. Though they are complete opposites, they get along peacefully, and that says a lot about the way they were raised. I love having Jonathan around and couldn't be more thrilled that he will join us in a month or so. Jane decides to call Jonathan to catch him up, and I decide to call home to see how the new puppy, Finley, is doing. That makes me smile as I recall a recent post I saw where it compares how spouses are treated vs. dogs when one leaves the house for work:

> *To the dog: "Who's gonna miss me? Give me kisses! Are you a good boy?"*
>
> *To the husband: "Bye."*

I would have never thought that I would be that person with a dog, but Finley has my heart already. After proper catch-ups with our families, Jane and I head to the veranda to sip on the champagne before showering. Hawaii. My once home. You are beautiful. We sit in silence for a good long time until I break it with an attempt to call Ginny's cell again. Still no answer. I can see on Jane's face that same tinge of concern she showed earlier at Ginny's house. There has to be an explanation. We decide to keep any concerns at bay until tomorrow. Tomorrow, if no contact, we will definitely need to do some poking around. With that, I jump up and head to the bathroom for a long shower. I can't wait to wear my new lime green dress. GG better be prepared for how hot Jane looks in her aqua blue dress. I chuckle at myself. I sound like a teenager. Carly would have given me the biggest eye roll if she was here. Shoot, I forgot to tell Tom to make sure the housekeeper is monitoring her makeup before leaving the house. Who knows what she will try to get away with while I am gone.

Chapter 13

Dylan – aka GG

Keeping this undercover identity has not been difficult so far. My role in my father's company is very behind the scenes, so it made sense when my father wanted to go undercover to discover what has been transpiring in our private jet company that he chose me. I have been tucked away, managing the operations of our fleet of jets, and have been out of the social scene for over six months since my wife decided to up and leave me for our EVP of Sales, Troy. Thankfully, we have no children, so good riddance. Large sums of money are pending, and we have been unable to reach the clients associated with the flights. It's always the same excuse: we should expect the wire transfer any day now, or there must be a mix-up at the bank with my card; all excuses that we have heard time and time again from clients, but generally, the payment eventually comes through. However, in the last year over $3 million in flights are pending payment. After Troy's departure, we discovered that Troy had a direct hand in bringing these particular clients on board, and all flights were handled by the crew I am flying with. Nathan, the other flight attendant, seems to be pretty tight-lipped, but since our travelers are two very beautiful women, he spent quite a hefty sum at one of the men's stores to spruce up his clothing. How can he afford a Tom Ford suit on his salary? Cocktails should loosen him up tonight as we enjoy our passengers' company.

The one, Jane, is stunning. You can tell she runs as her physique is slender but cut. I have to keep my wits about me to ensure that I handle the task at hand, but I am distracted. These women are on an adventure of a lifetime, and I am along for the ride! I run my fingers through my hair in frustration. Jane is going to have to wait. Getting Nathan to talk is my number one priority. The pilot is also going to have to wait as he did not join us at the hotel. He has family on the island, which he opted to visit. It's a bit odd as he has a very distinct Bostonian accent, and I thought I overheard him mention to Nathan that all of his family is back East, which he plans on visiting after this trip is over.

After a brief update to my father, I head toward the bathroom for a quick shower but stop short as there is a knock at the door. "Hey Dylan, you decent? Let's raid your mini bar before we head down to meet the ladies," Nathan shouts from the other side of the door. I open the door, which whisks a scent of cologne from Nathan that was overpowering. "Jesus, man, did you pour the whole bottle on you," I ask, holding my nose as to prevent any further intake. Nathan smirks while letting himself in and heads straight for the mini bar. "Go right ahead. I'm going to jump in the shower, and then I'll join you," I say, gesturing towards the minibar. I grab my briefcase and head to the bathroom. Nathan didn't seem to notice. I have a feeling Nathan is going to crack like an egg in no time, but I need to time it right so that no suspicion is raised to the pilot, and I get his involvement, if any, as well.

Nathan had made himself at home on the veranda and, by the looks of it, he is at least two mini bottles of vodka in already. I pour myself a tonic as I need to keep my wits about me and join him on the veranda. "This is the life, man, isn't it? Traveling like this never gets old," Nathan says with a big sigh and a chuckle. "Is this your first flight with Jet World? You seemed a bit green during service," he goes on. I will have to be careful in my response. "Yeah. I come from the hotel business, which included some day flights with clients as needed. Glad I have you on board to show me the ropes." That ought to feed his ego. As if on cue, he responds, "It's a good thing you're flying with me then. I am the best they've got, and depending on how you do, you may find this job is more than you had imagined." There you have it. My first potential lead into what's been going on. I decide not to push it so as not to raise any suspicion. Feeding into his ego again, I say, "Kate seems to be into you, man. You gonna go for it?" Nathan pounds back another vodka and raises his glass to me in cheers to confirm his intent. Poor guy. He must not have paid attention to the details on the flight roster as Kate is the married one. Yup, he is gonna be an easy one to get information out of. We finish our drinks and head out towards the Waterman Bar to meet the ladies. This is definitely the distraction I need after my hellish divorce.

Chapter 14

Jane

Drinks followed by dinner with "the stewards" was a blast, though Nathan (we now know his name) is certainly full of himself. He can't really pull off Tom Ford and the cologne! Way over the top. He is all into Kate, and Kate, God bless her, is flirting back, but she clearly draws the line when things start to get a little too friendly. Nathan is quite intoxicated, so he barely takes the hint, but his eyes soon drift, and before we know it, he is nowhere to be found.

GG is charming but reserved. He keeps a close eye on Nathan, watching his every move. There seems to be a story there, which I plan to explore as this trip progresses. Kate grows weary and decides to head back to the room, leaving GG and me alone in the restaurant, which is almost empty. In true Kate fashion, she leaves me with a wink and a nudge. Really Kate? We are too old for this shit, I say to myself.

GG and I decide to further our conversation at the hotel lounge for a nightcap. The atmosphere is perfect and not crowded so we seat ourselves in two comfortable chairs and order drinks. GG seems a bit distracted as he continues to look around, presumably for Nathan. "Are you concerned your flight buddy got himself in trouble?" I inquire. GG blushes and runs his fingers through his beautiful, thick, dark brown wavy hair. "Well, Nathan is pretty intoxicated. I should probably check on him when I head back to the room. Who knows when you ladies will want to take off again, so we really shouldn't be indulging too much. Hope this is not too forward, but you look amazing in that dress," he says. Now, it is my turn to blush. "Thanks," I respond as I take a large sip from my cosmopolitan. "We splurged a bit in one of the on-site boutiques. Kate, who normally does not shop, really enjoyed splurging with her new-found money." Shit, I probably shouldn't bring that up. GG doesn't seem to be affected by what I said. I quickly change the subject, "So Nathan, he's quite a character. He will soon learn Kate won't have it. Do you guys work together often?" GG wiggles a bit in his seat as if that was a bit of an uncomfortable question. "No, no. This is my first flight with him. I have a feeling I am going to have to babysit him a bit but don't worry. I will ensure he does not get out of line."

As I cross my legs, GG's eyes shift to my legs, staring intensely. My dress is a bit short, so my legs are in full view. As I reach for my glass he reaches for my hand and says, "Jane, you really do look beautiful tonight. I...." GG's sentence is interrupted by Nathan's loud voice yelling out GG's name as he stumbles towards us. That was my cue to head back to my room. GG will have to deal with him on his own. I give him a wink, explain my departure, and head out. We will have to put a pause on this until further notice. There is some mystery with GG that is intriguing. I wonder if Kate caught on to it.

I find Kate fast asleep as I look into her room from our adjoining bathroom. I gently close the door and get ready for bed. My mind shifts to Mark, which I quickly shut down, remembering Connie's words. Move on, Jane. Move on, Jane, I chant under my breath. This is going to be harder than I thought.

Chapter 15

Kate

I am up before my alarm, and so is Jane, so we decide to go for a quick run to keep our minds distracted until we can try to call Ginny again on her cell. We know her doctor's appointment is at 9 am, so we will try to call after 8 am, hoping to catch her before she leaves.

The beauty of Oahu is indescribable. One could try but could never give it justice. Jane and I jog in silence, taking it all in. She had already filled me in on her interrupted evening with GG. Nathan was certainly getting annoying before he scurried off, so I can only imagine how bad he was when he returned. I will have to keep an eye on that and maybe not include both of them, as I had. Though GG seems perfectly capable of handling him, I don't want it to become something we have to deal with. As we round the corner near the pool that we enjoyed yesterday, I hear Jane take a deep breath in, and she nudges me. Not far ahead of us is GG, running without a shirt on. Nice. We decide not to call out to him, so we turn and run in another direction. Clearly, Jane is not over-eager, and frankly, my mind is on Ginny today. We will have plenty of time to get this romance going between Jane and GG.

We grab lattes, a croissant, and some fruit and head back to our rooms, as it is a little after 8 am. Jane is the first to pull out her phone and ring Ginny. Again, no answer. Bewildered, she looks at her phone to make sure she rang the right number. We contemplate calling the neighbor to see if she had seen or heard anything but decide that if she had, she would have called us. This is beyond bizarre. I doubt Ginny is already at the doctor's office with her phone turned off. Just as we are contemplating what to do, my phone rings. It is Ginny's neighbor, Mrs. Hawksworth, calling. Mrs. H. for short. "Hello, Mrs. H. Okay if I call you Mrs. H.? This is Kate. Did Ginny and Gerald come home yesterday or call?" I ask. That was probably a dumb question; otherwise, we would have received a call. "Kate," Mrs. H. responds, "I have some disturbing news. It was too late for me to call you last night, but at around 10 pm, Oahu police came to our door to ask about Ginny and Gerald. They indicated that their car has been sitting at the base of the ridge for several weeks, which is unusual, so they ran the plates and came to their house to see if they were home. Not finding them there, they knocked on my door. Oh, Kate, I am worried now. What do you think we should do?" Jane sees my expression change and points to my phone to put Mrs. H. on speaker. "Mrs. H., this is Jane. I am here with Kate. Tell us again exactly what the officer said."

Mrs. H. relays again that the officers informed her that cars are monitored at the base of the ridge. They explained to her that cars typically come and go throughout the day, though sometimes cars linger for a day or even a week if the owners decide to camp. They apologized for being a bit behind following up on cars left at the ridge as they had other pressing matters. When they circled back yesterday morning, Ginny's car was still there. Their initial thought was that maybe the car was stalled, so the owners got picked up by someone else. That is why they came to Ginny's house last night to rule out this option. After learning that Ginny and Gerald have not been seen in weeks, they relay that a pretty rough storm came through about a week ago, which caused flooding and mudslides. They are now concerned that Ginny and Gerald might have gotten stuck somewhere out on the ridge and noted that, at first light, they are going to set out a search party. Moanalua Middle Ridge trail is only about a 12-mile round trip hike, but there are patches where the trails are rough with no coverage areas in sight. If they got caught in the rain and did not have a place to shelter...Mrs. H.'s voice began to trail and waiver as she utters their last words. They may have gotten washed down the ridge.

Jane and I look at each other in disbelief. We know from Ginny that Gerald is an expert hiker, so it is hard to imagine that they would get stuck on the ridge if a storm was coming. I finally speak and say, "Mrs. H., I am sure there is a reasonable explanation. You sit tight. Jane and I will drive over there and check in with the officers or search party. It is plenty early so we could do the hike ourselves if we need to. We promise to report back to you as soon as we have an update." "Bless you, girls. That would be great. Do be careful, and I will wait for your call," says Mrs. H. We bid each other goodbye, and I remind Mrs. H. that cell service might be difficult at the ridge but not to worry. We will get back to her.

We hang up and immediately begin to move about the suite in preparation. Jane and I brought appropriate enough gear for the hike, thank goodness. I call our car service, who is waiting for us as we exit the hotel. As we are about to load up into the car, GG steps in sight. "Hi, where are you ladies off to in such a hurry?" he asks. Jane steps towards him and explains the situation. He offers to help and hurries off to his room to change. We are glad to have him along for an extra set of eyes.

When we arrive at Moanalua Valley Park, which is where the trek begins and the cars park, it is clear that a search is already in progress. There are even news crews setting up, reporting live. Jane and I introduce ourselves to the officers while GG hangs back. They point out Ginny and Gerald's car, which we recognize immediately. I smile, remembering the countless times Ginny drove us to various points on the island to train. She felt from a conditioning standpoint, we should run on different terrains. We are told that the search started about an hour ago, so we tell them that we will hike the trail ourselves to help. They did not think it was necessary, but we tell them that we could not just sit around and do nothing. GG is already at the base of the trail, though I almost didn't recognize him with his hat and sunglasses on. I quickly call Mrs. H. to give her a quick update before we set out. Though I am happy to be in this beautiful spot again, concern looms over us as we begin. There has to be a reasonable explanation. There just has to be.

Chapter 16

Nathan

Where in the hell is Dylan? I saw him go out for a run from my window, but after several attempts to reach him with no success, I decide to wander the hotel. My head is pounding from last night. The last thing I remember is seeing Jane and Dylan all cozy in the hotel lounge. Dylan's dreaming if he thinks he is going to get any action with her. She is way out of his league. I wonder what Kate got up to last night? I thought she was into me, but that was probably the alcohol talking. I guess Dylan must have gotten me back to the room. He's probably gonna be pissed about that. He better not say anything to Randy.

I grab a double espresso shot from the on-ground Black Rifle Coffee Company and head out to the pool where we hung out yesterday. As I pull up a lounge chair and settle in, my phone rings. It is Randy; probably checking in to see if our clients have set a departure date/time for our second leg. Randy is an ass but a great pilot. He trusts me to keep my mouth shut when we have Troy's bidding to carry out. Randy had a meeting with Troy last night to catch up as there have been recent inquiries on certain flights that we managed, as payment has not come through to the jet company. No kidding. Payments are going to Troy, rather, which aren't traceable as all paid in cash. These "clients" fly under pseudonyms and identification, all arranged by Troy. What's in it for these "clients?" They are able to handle their unscrupulous affairs undercover. Troy has assured us that this would never be traced back to any of us. I smirk at our scam of all scams and answer, "Randy, what's up? Calling to check up on us? I'm just lounging by the...." "Jesus, Nathan. You sound hung over. What did Troy tell us about partying while on a job? Doesn't matter if it's one of his or regular. We have to be steady and consistent in our approach to not raise any suspicion. You guys probably shouldn't have taken the offer to stay at our client's hotel. Fill me in," demands Randy. "Look, Randy, there is no reason to get all fatherly with me. All is well here, though Dylan seems to have disappeared. He was hanging pretty late with one of them, but she left ahead of us. He isn't answering his phone, so I am just now walking around to find him," I responded in annoyance. "More importantly, how did the convo go with Troy? Is he getting any more inquiries from corporate?" I am not in the mood for this, as my head is still pounding. I go on, "Look, Randy, if you have nothing to report, I am going to keep walking around to see if I can find Dylan. The ladies have not given us any thoughts on when we might head out. Apparently, their visit yesterday did not go as planned, so they are back out again today." "Just keep things cool and professional, Nathan. We can't raise any suspicion. Keep an eye on Dylan, and keep your mouth shut," says Randy.

Rather than argue, I give him what he wants and hang up. I'd better drink some water and take a few Tylenol before continuing my hunt for Dylan. The sun is already intense and is making me feel pretty nauseous. Not cool that Dylan is not answering his phone. He knows the drill of always being available. *"Guess I'm going to have to pull a Randy on Dylan when I see him,"* I chuckle to myself. Just before heading back to my room, I check with the front desk to see if they know the whereabouts of the ladies or Dylan. Looks like they left the hotel with Dylan. Why would Dylan be going with them? I try his phone again. This time, it immediately goes to voicemail. Now I'm pissed. "Dylan, what the hell, man? You need to answer your phone when either Randy or I call. Where did you guys go? Call me as soon as you pick up this message," I say. Well, I have done my duty. Might as well relax and enjoy paradise. Rather than get Tylenol, I decide to head back out to the pool and have a Bloody Mary. Screw Randy and Dylan. I've got nothing to do but sit and wait, so I might as well enjoy myself.

Chapter 17

Ginny

The pain in my knee is agonizing. I know the fall has caused a periprosthetic fracture to my knee replacement, and I haven't been able to stand for several days due to the pain. Gerald is in much worse shape with what we suspect to be a fractured clavicle, and his tibia is clearly broken, as it has broken through the skin. I was able to reach him in the first couple of days to stop the bleeding and somewhat hold the bones in place. He is experiencing severe swelling, and it looks like infection has set in. I need to get him medical attention soon, but how?

We knew the storm was coming. We could tell by the skyline. When we were just 2 miles from the entrance, the storm hit with a vengeance as we teetered in the middle of sharp-angled drop-offs on either side. Our shoes could no longer grip as mudslides set in. Wind was whipping, and we knew there were ropes that we could hold onto, but we could not see them through the rain.

I tumbled first and fell down the slope, grasping for anything I could grab onto. When my fall finally stopped, I yelled for Gerald but heard nothing in return. Then I saw him. Sliding down past me on a bit steeper part. He landed no more than 12 feet from me by grabbing onto a tree root.

Since then, we have been lying here in our own filth, eating the remains of our provisions, which are now completely gone. We didn't bring flares. Didn't even cross our mind when we were packing. Our cell phones were long dead, though I am sure we would not be able to get any reception on this side of the ridge.

Though I don't think Gerald suffered any head trauma, I made sure to balance his sleep and consciousness. I try to keep things light, asking if this is the adventure, he had imagined for us after my retirement. He would never admit that we are too old for this. Shit just happens, and it could happen to anyone. That's not what my knees are telling me, but I keep that thought to myself.

As I shift to take the pressure off of my right hip, I see a flash of light coming and going across the ridge. *Am I seeing things?* I squint, then refocus. Nothing. Must be a reflection of something. I hear a very faint chopping noise almost immediately after but can't make it out. I can hear Gerald mutter what sounds like "helicopter." The noise grows louder and louder – chakk-chackk-chak-chak, chak-a-chak-akk-chk-chk-chk. Far away, I can see what looks like a helicopter, which appears to be scanning the ridge up and down. Finally, the hope of a rescue is in sight. I reach into my backpack for a red zip-up that I have. I want it close so that I can begin to wave it as soon as the helicopter gets closer. It is up to me to make sure we get out of this, and when we do, Gerald will hear it from me. We have to be realistic about what we can do physically, at our age. I prop myself up and wait, keeping my eyes locked on the helicopter.

Chapter 18

Jane

The first three miles are an easy walk into Kamananui Valley, which leads us to a network of trails where we make our initial ascent. After about a half an hour, we scale the first hump, which gives us our first elevated view of the valley's treetops sprawling out beneath us. I had forgotten about the ropes, which were now visible, that we would need to use as we headed up steep sections. I try to imagine walking this during a storm, with torrential rain and wind. What were Ginny and Gerald thinking? GG breaks the silence as he peers down the steep drops on either side. "Have mercy, this is sketchy. You say that your friends are an older couple? They must really be in good physical shape to take this on." Just as he says that, I brace myself against the bark of a tree to keep from losing my balance. "Shit, this is sketchier than I remember. Kate and I have done this ridge more than once, but I think we were better equipped," I respond. Kate does not respond as she was ahead of us, peering up and down the rugged spine, looking for any clue as to where Ginny and Gerald were. Two helicopters were circling the ridge above us, but it seems as though they were giving up as we see them head towards the park entrance. God forbid if they had tumbled down the ridge. How would we even find them? I could see the worry on

Kate's face and knew we wouldn't stop until we reached the end of the trail.

After a few hours in, we reach the end of the trail and catch a sliver of the Pacific Ocean. We reach Kate, and she turns to me with tears in her eyes and says, "Oh, Jane, where do you think they are? We've walked the full ridge. Helicopters don't appear to have found them. I thought we would have found search crews all over this but we haven't seen one." The three of us stand there, find our center of gravity, and take a seat. "Kate, let's take a moment. Hydrate. I am sure we missed something along the trail. I suspect they were heading back when the storm hit, so the view back might be where we might find a clue. Let's take it slow and focus our search with you on the right, me on the left, and GG, I mean Dylan, you can support either side," I suggest. GG looks at me inquisitively, but I brush it off as my eyes dart to Kate. Not registering, Kate nods and takes a handkerchief that GG offers, and wipes her eyes. As she hands it back to him, I catch a glimpse of the initials AD embroidered on a corner. AD? A, who knows? D, for Dylan? Seems there continues to be more to his story, but will have to leave it for now. Kate is already up and itching to start back. Taking the clue, GG and I get up, and we three start the trek back at a slower pace, scouring the landscape below us.

Chapter 19

Ginny

As the helicopter looms over us, I begin to wave my red jacket madly. It feels like it weighs a ton of bricks as it is still wet from the downpour, but I muster all the strength I have to keep waving it in the air. I scream "help" until I am hoarse but the noise from the propellers is too loud and drowns me out. In what seems like only seconds, the helicopter is right above us, then gone. Gerald moans, signaling me that this is impossible. We are positioned where the ridge dips slightly inward, and with all of the foliage around, it is difficult to be spotted without some sort of flare.

It is clear that the helicopter is searching for us, so it is known that we have gone missing. I bet Jamie (Mrs. H.) is going out of her mind with worry. I start to panic as the helicopter moves out of sight. "Gerald, you with me? The helicopter is gone but don't you worry. That is a sign that they know we are missing. It will only be a matter of time," I say, half believing my words. For Gerald's sake, I am trying to stay convincingly positive, but I am beginning to panic. I don't think Gerald is going to last another night with nothing to treat his fever that has set in and has not let up.

After about an hour, I hear Gerald moan what I think is the word "listen." Could he hear something?

"What's that, Gerald? Did you hear something?" I say. Again, he mutters, "Just listen."

Chapter 20

Kate

I am responsible for the right side of the ridge, so with every step, I scour the ground and then peer over the ridge as much as I can without toppling over. I can see Jane doing the same, and Nathan is walking behind us, looking both ways. I know we were about 2.5 miles away from the trail entrance with nothing in sight. I trudge along as panic begins to set in. I stop to take a drink of water, which halts GG who is directly behind me, causing him to lose footing and slide slightly on the loose terrain beneath us. He is quick enough to grab onto one of the ropes and is able to hoist himself up. "Jesus, Dylan. I should have given you some warning. Are you alright?" I ask. GG is rummaging in the soil beneath his feet, and after about a minute, he lifts a small object up in the air, brushing off the dirt, and then he hands it to me. "Check this out. Looks like a University pin – The University of Hawaii," he reads. Jane backtracks carefully to where I am standing and we both stare at the pin together. "You're right, Dylan! This is actually a pin that only coaches wear at the University. Holy shit. Could this be Ginny's pin?" I ask. "This has to be hers. She has to be close. Jane, what should we do?" I ask, slightly hysterical. I begin to scream out Ginny and Gerald's names, confident they will respond. Jane and GG join me as we repeat their names in unison. We scream until our voices begin to sound hoarse, stopping in between to listen for any sort of response. Nothing.

Jane then moves over to the right side and peers over the ridge. "We could use the ropes and work our way down, but we have no idea if this is exactly where they are. Nor do we know which side of the ridge they would be on. We need help to cover this area before nightfall and now we have a clue as to where they might be. Let me think. How about I head back to the entrance..." Jane's sentence trails off as Dylan points to a group of people coming up the trail. They appear to be part of the search and rescue team that we met at the entrance. "Hey, hi! Over here! We found something!" I shout.

We fill the search and rescue team in on the significance of our finding and they immediately spring into action, using their digital two-way radios to inform the team at the base and to inform the helicopters of our location so that they can search the area again. We know that we have to step aside and let them do their thing, So, following the advice of the rescue team—though hesitant—we return to the base, where the trail begins, to wait.

When we finally get on solid ground, I lunge for GG and give him a big hug. "Dylan, we are so thankful you were with us and found the pin. Without the sequence of events that happened, we would have come up empty-handed, and who knows if we would have ever found our beloved Ginny and her husband. At least now we have a chance. Oh, and maybe soon we will tell you why Jane called you GG," I proclaim mischievously as I look at Jane, who is blushing and proceeds to give me the evil eye. GG blushes and pulls away, noting that he is happy to help and is relieved there is hope now in finding them. Jane also gives him a hug, but this time, he does not pull back as quickly.

We finally have cell service, so while Jane calls our driver, I call Mrs. H. to fill her in. She cries and cries as I promise her that as soon as I have more news, I will ring her back. Jane has asked the driver to run and fetch food and drink for about 20 people, which should cover us and the rescue team. We know we'll be here for the long haul so we better get nourished. This is the first time I smile today, knowing that Ginny and Gerald have to be alright.

"Jane. Would you mind asking the driver not to leave yet? I need to get a ride back to the hotel to check in with Nathan. He has left several messages and has spoken with our pilot, so I'd better contact both of them. Will you guys be okay on your own?" asks GG. "No problem, Dylan. We will be fine. Start heading back to the entrance while I call the driver. We will text you as we find out more," responds Jane, almost sounding disappointed. I thank him again and usher him off, saying, "Just tell the driver to keep the food and drinks fresh, and we will come down once we hear back from the rescue team. See you soon, Dylan." I take a deep breath and pull off my backpack to find something to sit on. I am dead dog tired from the hike and emotional day. Jane and I sit down in silence and finally take the time to look at the beauty around us.

Chapter 21

Ginny

I am listening for what seems like an hour, but in reality, it really has only been about 15 minutes. I hear again the pulse of the helicopter blades, which is growing louder and louder. I grab my red zip-up and begin to wave it again. The wind force around us begins to gain as the helicopter draws near, and then there it is, hovering right above us. I know they have now seen us, and I cry out to Gerald, "I think we have been found! Gerald, do you hear me?" He doesn't respond, but I can still see his chest moving up and down.

Off in the distance, I see one of the ropes I couldn't reach begin to move.   Was that just the wind from the helicopter causing it to move? I shift my eyes between the helicopter and the rope, feeling a bit helpless as I can't move. As the rope continues to move, I start to see dirt falling from above. This could only mean that someone is up there taking the rope down. I muster up all the energy I can and begin to yell out, "Help! Help! Help! We are down here! Help!" Then I see him. A rescue team member is maneuvering himself down the rope towards us.

The team works fast to get to us safely, first holstering us, then hoisting us up to the helicopter. I am so relieved, but I am shaking with shock. Thankfully, the helicopter is equipped to provide Gerald with some quick medical attention while they transport him to where the ambulance is waiting. Gerald is the first to be moved and is quickly settled into the ambulance. As I am being carried off of the ambulance, I catch a glimpse of two people waving my way. My jaw drops as they come into focus, and I realize it is Kate and Jane. Wait - what? Am I dreaming? Why are they here? They approach me and grab my hands while Kate says with tears in her eyes, "Oh Ginny, we were so worried, but then we found your pin, and here you are." She isn't making any sense, which Jane senses and says, "Ginny, never mind that. Let's get you both to the hospital and then we will have a proper debrief when you are able. We are just so happy to see you."

These girls standing before me are a highlight in my long coaching career. I am so grateful to see their bright and shining faces. I squeeze their hands back and rest my head against the stretcher, shutting my eyes as relief takes over me. We are safe. Gerald will be fine. He's going to get an earful from me when he is better.

Chapter 22

Jane

Kate and I sprint back to the park entrance after the rescue crew informed us that they had found Ginny and Gerald and are transporting them to the entrance, where the ambulance is waiting for them. Much to my surprise GG is there, with our driver and the much-needed food. We update GG on what has transpired, and he flashes a smile that is swoonworthy. My God, he is gorgeous and I am sure I am looking pretty beaten up right now.

Kate cannot contain her excitement and chatters on and on long after Ginny and Gerald are transported to Kuakini Medical Center. We let Ginny know that we would come to the hospital tomorrow, giving them a chance to settle in and get seen and treated by the medical team. We hand out the food our driver had picked up, then climb into the car to head back to the hotel for a much-needed bath and cocktail.

"Dylan, were you able to connect with Nathan and Randy? Is there any issue?" Kate asks. "Oh yeah, no. Nathan was just concerned because he could not reach me while we had no service on the ridge. I found him sleeping by the pool, so I knew there was no issue. I guess Randy called to check in is all. We should give him an update on when you might think we will depart for Virginia," says GG.

"Honestly, Dylan, I expect we will be here at least another day or two to make sure Ginny and Gerald are okay. I won't be able to enjoy the rest of my trip without knowing that," says Kate. "I agree," I say. "Just let Randy know that we will give him 24 hours' notice as soon as we check in with Ginny tomorrow. Does that work?" GG nods and assures us that he will provide both Randy and Nathan with the update.

We ride the rest of the way back to the hotel in silence until Kate jumps up and says, "Shit, I need to call Mrs. H. to give her an update. How could I have forgotten?" I give GG a smile and pat Kate on the knee as if to say, go right ahead. I can hear Mrs. H. crying through the phone, but happy tears for sure. Though Kate tells her that it would probably not be a good idea to go to the hospital tonight, she insists and says she will stay there until we arrive tomorrow. Ginny sure is lucky to have such a wonderful neighbor.

I can feel GG's knee pressed up against me, which makes me blush. It was nice to be close to him, feeling the heat from his body. As if he knew what I was thinking, he glances over and gives me another of his smiles. Oh boy, I am in trouble. I am clearly smitten with him, which is a strange feeling I have not felt in a very long time. As we approach the hotel, I quickly adjust myself so that we are no longer touching and begin to rummage through my backpack looking for God knows what. Oh right. The room key. Got it.

Kate and I grunt as we pull ourselves out of the car, weary from today's activity. "Dylan, again, we can't thank you enough. I think we are going to call it a night and just order room service. Get some rest, and we will update you tomorrow after our hospital visit," I say. With a bewildered look, GG bids us goodbye and heads into the hotel. Kate punches my arm and says, "What the heck Jane? We're gonna order room service? What's that all about?" "I'm exhausted, Kate. I just want to hang in the room with you, have a cocktail, and order some room service. It's been a long day and anyway, don't you need to catch up with your family? I think we have had enough adventure for one day," I say. "Fine. I'll give you a pass for tonight, but I won't give you a pass to pass on what is happening with GG. Speaking of, we should probably fill him in on what GG stands for or at least stop using it between us so that we don't let it slip again!" Kate exclaims. We laugh, grab each other's arm, and head to our room, walking in step the whole way. I love our friendship and am so glad we have this amazing opportunity to do this together. We throw our things down in our room, and Kate makes a beeline to the mini-fridge. Good Ol' Kate A woman after my own heart.

Chapter 23

Kate

All is good at home, thank God. Tom reports that they have all settled into a routine with Ms. Susan, the caregiver and Ms. Emily, the housekeeper/cook. Jackson is taking the new protocol like a champ and is feeling much better. So much so that Tom thinks he might want to go out for track in the Fall. That's my boy. Jackson's first blood draw since starting the new protocol of medicine is next week, so Tom promises to update me as soon as he has the results. The kids pop Finley into the FaceTime video so that I can see his adorable face. He is going to be so big by the time I get home. When it is just Tom and me again, I remember to tell him to keep an eye on Carly, to make sure she is not leaving the house with makeup. "Let Ms. Emily know too, Tom, because I know you will be too preoccupied to get a good look at her," I say with a smirk on my face. Tom sighs, then nods, taking my neurosis like a champ. "You just worry about you and your matchmaking. I've got this under control," replies Tom. After several air kisses, we bid each other goodbye, and I settle into my bed for the night. Jane has long gone to bed after we devoured burgers, fries, and cocktails.

It feels like I have only been asleep for 5 minutes when Jane comes busting through my door. "Kate, are you going to sleep all day? I've already been for a run! Let's get dressed and get to the hospital. I already have the driver queued up and I grabbed you some breakfast. Come on! Moooove!" Jane says as she pounces on my bed. Jane has already talked to Mrs. H., who has been with Ginny all night. Mrs. H. reported that both Ginny and Gerald, though dehydrated, were doing well despite their injuries. Gerald was immediately given antibiotics for the infection, and surgery is scheduled for this morning to set up his broken tibia and close the wound. Thankfully, his fractured clavicle will not require surgery, but he will have to wear a sling for some time. Ginny did indeed have a fracture to her knee replacement, which would require surgery to fix. They are going to need some serious help as they heal and undergo physical therapy. We are talking for at least a couple of months. I will make sure they both have the necessary care before we leave. I can't have Ginny worrying about a thing post-retirement. After everything she has done for me and Jane, we owe her. I won't take no for an answer. Jane nods in agreement and gives me a big hug in thanks.

We arrive at the hospital just as Gerald is being wheeled back for surgery. Mrs. H. gives us both a big hug and leaves us to be with our mentor. Our friend. Despite everything, Ginny looks bright-eyed and raring to go. "Girls, what the heck? I thought I was delirious when I saw you yesterday but Jaime confirmed I wasn't and filled me in on why you are here. Is this true, Kate? Did you really inherit a fortune, so now the both of you are going to be gallivanting all over the place on a private jet?" says Ginny. "Ginny, yes, it is unbelievably true. Just the two of us and, well, a really hot steward, but we will get into that later. Ginny, let me return the 'what the heck?' What happened?" I say.

After several hugs, we settle in to hear Ginny recount what happened, starting with her departure from the University of Hawaii. We apologize for not being aware, as we would have certainly made the trip to attend her retirement party. She waves us off as if it was no big deal. Apparently, it was just a small gathering of staff and athletes at Ginny's request. "Mark my words; when Gerald is lucid enough to understand me, he is going to get an earful from me. We are not in our 20s anymore, and we should not be taking on sketchy hikes, especially with my knees. I don't think he will ever grow up," Ginny says with exasperation. Both Jane and I laugh out loud because we know Gerald well, and he will never settle down, so Ginny has a battle on her hands. "Ginny, you might have to play up your injury to garner enough sympathy from Gerald or simply say you aren't going! I don't think he will go without you," says Jane. Ginny is the love of Gerald's life, and though he might be a bit self-involved, he would do anything for Ginny. "I don't suspect either of you will be climbing any mountains anytime soon so take advantage of this time to reality check Gerald. You certainly don't want to slow him down because remaining active is so important," Jane says, reflecting on her own parents. Her dad remained active until the bitter end and lived well beyond his cardiologists' expectations. Her mother, on the other hand, snubbed her nose at exercise, and though she lived a good long time, once she got sick, she was gone within months.

As Jane is reminiscing about her parents, Gerald is wheeled in from surgery. Ginny and Gerald are lucky enough to get roomed together. The surgeon reports that they were able to repair the fracture with intramedullary nailing (inserting a metal rod and screwing it to the bone).

The recovery for the fracture is three to six months and as the surgeon reports this, we both look at Ginny and wink. "Doctor Andrews, when will you be repairing Ginny's knee replacement? It would be great if they could recover together, which, by the way, I will be paying for where insurance does not pick up," I say. "Kate, now just wait one minute. You will do no such thing….," Ginny says, trying to pipe in. "Ginny, your words are useless to me. I have already made up my mind, and I have money to spend, so that is the end of the discussion," I say as I cross my arms as if in a tantrum. Ginny rolls her eyes and looks over at Jane who simply smirks as if to say, no sense in arguing with her. The doctor is kind enough to wait for our banter to cease and responds, "We will get Ginny in the day after tomorrow, and I expect recovery time will be similar to Gerald's. We will be sending them both to rehab before returning home, but it would be great if they can have some assistance when they return home to continue outpatient rehab." Kate nods her head and lets the doctor know she is on it and will arrange all. As we wrap things up with the doctor, Gerald is coming to, so we say our goodbyes, give Gerald a peck on the head, and head for the door, letting Ginny know we will be back tomorrow to check in on them before we continue on our adventure. Jane and I are both disappointed that we cannot spend more time with them, drinking Ginny's famous cocktails, but we are both relieved that they will be okay. "Girls, I can't tell you how overjoyed I am to see you. Tomorrow, I want to hear all about what you two have been up to. I need pictures!" Ginny demands as we step into the hallway. "You got it, Ginny!" we respond in unison as we exit the room, blowing her air kisses.

On the ride back to the hotel, we discuss our plan for departure and decide that our time in Virginia will be short, barring any unexpected adventures like we encounter in Hawaii. Ginny informs us that two of her sons will fly in to be with her during surgery and transition to rehab for both of them, so that is one less thing we have to worry about. I obtain all the necessary numbers so that we can stay in contact, and I can arrange for any payments needed. I chuckle at Ginny's tantrum when I informed her, I was paying, but it was our turn to take care of her. It made me so happy to be able to do this for her.

With a burst of energy, Jane says, "Let's go to the beach! North Shore specifically. I want to see some crazy big waves before we go, and this is the perfect time of the year for them. No need to go to the hotel just yet, right?" She holds her hand up for a high five, which I reciprocate. I can certainly use a strong Waialua coffee from the coffee mill, and there is something humbling about viewing gigantic waves. "What about GG? Won't he wonder where you are?" I ask mischievously. Jane just rolls her eyes, gives me a shut the fuck up look, and grabs 2 small bottles of prosecco from the refrigerator. Appears drinking is in order. Why the hell not?

Chapter 24

Dylan

GG? What could that possibly stand for and why have they given me a nickname? Giving someone a secret nickname usually means something negative, but since they called it out and are going to tell me what it stands for, it can't be bad. Can it? Let's hope it's something like "gorgeous guy," not "gifted guy." Neither of them seem catty, so I am sure it stands for something positive. I'll go with that.

Kate had called Randy to inform him of their desired departure time, which will be tomorrow afternoon. I don't expect we will see them before we leave, which gives me a sense of disappointment. That can't be appropriate. I know I am on this trip for a purpose, but I never expected to meet two fun-loving women that I feel comfortable around.

With the departure time set, it is time for Randy, Nathan, and me to get back to the jet to prepare. Nathan and Randy seem to be at odds, working in silence mostly, with an occasional order barked from Randy. Nathan did vent to me earlier that Randy was being a bit of an ass when he spoke to him last. Randy did give me a bit of a tongue-lashing for being uncontactable for a period of time. Still, when he heard me recount the recent adventure on the ridge of Moanalua Middle Ridge trail,

89

he backed off since I was assisting our clients. Nathan seems to be warming up to me, already sharing concerns that he has with Randy. Randy is going to be a tougher nut to crack, so I will need to work harder to get some one-on-one time with him. "Randy, how about we three catch dinner together tonight, somewhere outside of the hotel, since our clients are busy until we depart? I mean, hanging with just Nathan is great but I would be interested in hearing your tales of travel?" I ask as I glance at Nathan who smirks back at me. Randy abruptly answers in his thick Bostonian accent, "We can't. Nathan and I have other business to attend to, right Nathan? In fact, we are leaving directly from here, so sorry. You are going to have to dine alone." Nathan seems startled by that announcement, which was odd. What business could they possibly have since they are dedicated to this trip in its entirety? Nathan recovers and chimes in, "Yeah, sorry, Dylan. Duty calls," he responds. "No problem," I reply and ask, "How was your visit with your family, Randy?" Randy stares at me for a few seconds, then glances at Nathan and responds, "It was a pissah hanging with them. They are madly wicked I can't stay for longer."

Randy confirms that the flight time is approximately nine hours from Oahu to Virginia, and due to the size of the jet, we will not have to stop to fuel. Nathan and I work diligently to prepare the cabin and order the necessary provisions for the flight, then Nathan and Randy take off to handle their mysterious "business." I take the opportunity to check in with my father, informing him of their business comment. I have already checked the flight manifests, and nothing seemed out of the ordinary, with all flight payments cleared. There is a new pilot that had been brought on, referred to the company by Randy and though his background is stellar, there is reason to be cautious. "Alex, I know it has been rough for you, and now I have sent you on this assignment. See if you can take some pleasure in this particular trip since you will be visiting some beautiful places. Yes, we need to figure out this issue, but not at the risk of you finding a bit of joy," says my father. My father, though a tough businessman, is a gentle soul. He has been such a great mentor to so many, even Troy. His attrition rate at the company is 0%, other than Troy being fired. Bastard. My gut is telling me Nathan and Roger are deeply involved in Troy's schemes and will be joining Troy in prosecution once proven guilty. I think the key will be to stick closer to Randy, as he seems to act as the conduit.

We bid our goodbyes, and I Uber back to the hotel. The private car hasn't returned, so I am sure the ladies are enjoying themselves somewhere on this beautiful island. With nothing to do I decide to head to the pool to ponder my next moves. No rush. I will take my father's advice and try to enjoy myself. Randy, but more certainly, Nathan will slip up, and I will uncover their scheme. I am certain of that.

<h1 style="text-align:center">Chapter 25</h1>

<h1 style="text-align:center">Randy</h1>

Leg 2 – Virginia

Damn it. We barely have an overnight in Virginia before the ladies decide to move on to Paris. Totally hoses my meet-up with potential "clients" Troy had identified. Troy is just going to have to handle the details without me and bring Andy into the fold sooner, as Nathan and I need all eyes off of us for a while until the boss man comes to the realization that the losses cannot be recovered.

I can't get a good sense as to whether Dylan will be a good candidate for our schemes so I haven't brought it up to Troy yet. We need more hands-on deck. Dylan showed up out of nowhere to join us on this excursion, and with all the side hustle Troy has me doing, I haven't had a chance to scope Dylan out. It sure was a lot easier when Troy was on staff!

"Good morning, ladies. The weather today is perfect for flying, so it should be smooth sailing to Paris. Our flight time will be approximately eight hours, so please lay back, relax, and enjoy the meals Nathan and Dylan have in store for you. Do you have any questions before we take off," I ask. Kate responds, "Thanks, Randy. Please take your time. I haven't spent a minute looking at French, so I will need this flight time to study! Thank goodness for Duolingo." Jane chuckles and shakes her head to say no questions, so I turn around and head into the cockpit. I've never liked the sound of the French language. Too many silent letters and ambiguity in pronunciation. I took four years of it in college and I still can't speak a lick. It makes me really uncomfortable to ask a French person if they speak English. I usually get a piqued facial expression and a strong "no." Probably has to do with my Bostonian accent. Well, hopefully, the ladies won't linger for too long though, who knows what they will encounter once they connect with whomever they need to connect with. I don't know the full story, but apparently, Kate is new money rich, and it has something to do with someone in Paris. Ah, who cares? It's of no interest to me other than a possible sizable bonus at the end of the trip. I make a mental note to myself to make it clear to Troy when I speak to him next that my current clients ARE my priority because there is income to be had, and I need to do my best to secure the best outcome.

Nathan pops his head in to let me know that all cross checks are complete. Wheels up.

Chapter 26

Jane

GG, though still friendly and charming, seems to be distancing himself a bit. Not one glance my way from his perch in the galley. Kate is busy babbling in French as she zooms through the Duolingo app, so I am left to my thoughts. Paris is going to be hectic, so I am not sure if I will have the opportunity to get into his story a bit more. My mind drifts to the handkerchief he gave Kate at the ridge, which had the initials AD. I decide that there was no time like the present, so I beckon GG over and ask, "So Dylan, I am curious. At the ridge, you gave Kate your handkerchief, which I could not help but notice the initials AD embroidered on it. What does AD stand for? Is Dylan not your first name?" Dylan's eyes dart at Nathan, then back at me, and he answers, "Oh, that. It belonged to my grandfather, so those initials have no association with me." Nathan looks his way but does not seem to be interested in our conversation. Then Dylan leans forward and says quietly, "I will fill you in sometime soon when we are alone," and with that, he turns and heads back to the galley. He left both me and Kate with our jaws a bit dropped, and we turn to each other, puzzled as if to say, what could that be all about? Of course, Kate takes it with complete intrigue, which adds ammunition to her already brewing scheme. "Oh yeah, there's a story there, and I'll be damned if I don't get it out of him," Kate whispers to me. I elbow her to hush and point to her iPad to continue her learning. Kate flashes me a very large grin and returns to her French, "Pouvez-vous me dire où se trouve la salle de bains." Yikes, that accent does not sound right. I hope the French are patient people!

After a delicious wedge salad followed by a short rib pappardelle, Nathan serves us crème brulee, which is a popular French dessert. Yum. I just love the crunchy caramelized sugar on top of the luscious vanilla crème. Just goes so well having two contrasting layers. My heart twinges as I recall my mother preparing the same dessert for us when we were growing up. My brother always wanted to be the one that used the brulee torch to car-amelize. He always won that battle because I was not allowed to touch anything with a flame. Albeit a bit dra-matic, I did once leave candles burning on my parents' dining room table, which ruined the antique. A story I will never live down, even now, many years after my par-ents' passing. Jonathan loves to dredge up my faux pas – well, there is something I know in French – to see me squirm and get defensive. He always displays himself as mild-mannered and calm but he clearly has a mischie-vous side to him. I think that is why he and Kate get along so well. They are always torturing me when they are to-gether. *Hope that doesn't become a thing when he joins us in Egypt,* I think, then chuckle. Kate looks at me and asks, "What's going through your mind, Jane? Are you dreaming about a little passionate time with G squared? You know they say Paris is the most romantic city in the world. You can take a stroll arm-in-arm down the canal, or I heard they have covered passageways where you can sneak a kiss. Just saying." "Good God, Kate. I think you are getting ahead of yourself. He really isn't giving me the time of day, so this romance may be over before it even starts," I say with a glance GG's way. Kate frowns and whispers, "This romance is a go, so buckle up. I am going to be busy with my mom's uncle's executor, Delphine, so you will have plenty of time to explore the city. Please tell me you will take this opportunity to spend a little time with Dylan. He's just busy, and after all, he is working, so no childish tantrums from you, missy." She is right. I am being childish. I give my sweet friend a smile and recline my chair for a little nap. After all - children need naps!

Chapter 27

Kate

Leg 3 - Paris

Paris, nicknamed "the city of lights," is exquisite and charming. My appointment with Delphine Renault isn't until tomorrow, so Jane and I stroll along the Seine, taking in all the magnificent views. The weather is perfect this time of year, though a bit chilly, which we don't seem to mind as we walk arm in arm. Since we are staying close to the Louvre, we decide to tour the museum and then continue our sightseeing after my appointment with Delphine tomorrow.

I can't wait to be surrounded by original paintings from famous artists like Leonardo da Vinci, Rembrandt, and Rubens. It gives me chills to think that I am finally going to see the original Mona Lisa, as I have only seen replicas in books or on a postcard. Jane has been here before, so she is a great guide. She is fortunate to have traveled all over the world while her father was in the Foreign Service, so she is a plethora of knowledge as we walk the halls built for French Kings. I hang onto every word as Kate rambles on and on about Philip II, Francis I, and Henry IV who all play a role in constructing what stands today as the Louvre.

I know I have reached the Mona Lisa as there is a very large crowd surrounding it. It takes us a while to edge our way forward, but when we reach it, there she is, poised with her enigmatic smile. Jane tells me the tale of when the painting was stolen and thought lost forever. A Louvre worker simply hid it in his jacket and walked out with it with the goal of bringing it back to Italy. Its place of origin. Hard to imagine that he hid it in his apartment for two years until he tried to sell it, which led to him being caught.

After spending a solid hour admiring the Mona Lisa, we move on to where the famous statues of the Venus of Milo (represents Aphrodite – the goddess of love in Greek mythology) and the Winged Victory of Samothrace (commemorates the Greek victory in a sea battle) are. I can't take my eyes off either of them as they stand there in their glory. My thoughts are halted by a tap on my shoulder. I turn around and there is GG, standing beside Jane. How long have I been captivated that I did not notice them together? The dryness in my mouth tells me I must have been standing there in awe for some time with my mouth wide open, oblivious. "Look who had the same ideas as us, Kate," says Jane. Wait, is she blushing? What in the hell did I miss? "Well, hey, Dylan, quite a coincidence. Did you see the Mona Lisa yet? It's fabulous. We are about to head out for some dinner. Care to join us?" I ask. "Thanks, but I only have a little more time before I need to meet up with Randy and Nathan. I didn't want to miss the opportunity to see these two beauties while here," GG states. As I am about to mutter, "Aww, that's sweet," he points to the two statues. We chuckle as we catch on, then walk together towards the exit. "Dylan offered to escort me shopping tomorrow while you are tied up with the executor," Jane notes with a flicker of excitement. "Perfect! I wouldn't want you wandering on your own or spending too much money so Dylan, keep an eye on her," I say as I wink his way. "Yes, ma'am," he says with a salute then leaves me and Jane standing there in silence. When he is well out of sight, I yank on Jane's arm and insist on the details while I was apparently in La-La Land.

Chapter 28

Jane

The Hotel du Louvre is stunning. Kate directed Sasha to spare no expense, so she booked me the Pissarro Suite, which apparently once housed the painter Pissarro, who painted 11 masterpieces while living there. Kate is in the Palais Royal Suite, which is known for its outstanding views over the Louvre and the Palais-Royal. I am so happy to be back in Paris, and I cannot wait to hit the streets with GG. This will be interesting and hopefully not awkward because I don't want my time in Paris to be tainted. After a quick workout in the fitness center with Kate, I hurry down to the hotel lobby to meet GG.

GG is anxious to get going as he has never been to Paris before. I look at him sternly, noting I wasn't going anywhere until I had coffee and a croissant, so after walking around the Palais Royal – Musee du Louvre, we find a quaint café with outdoor seating. We settle in and sit in silence as we observe the hustle and bustle around us. I break the silence and say, "So, other than catering to my shopping needs, what do you have on your "must do" list while you are here in Paris?" I am surprised by his answer when he notes that he watches a lot of French and British period drama so he is dying to see Versailles. His point of reference is the series Versailles on Netflix, which makes me chuckle. "You won't be disappointed then when you visit Versailles because it is exactly as it is shown in that series. I, too, am a period drama junkie, so we have that in common," I respond, blushing a bit as I hint at our connection. GG stares long and hard at me, and then his stare is interrupted by our waitress bringing what we had ordered. We spend the rest of our time at the café discussing what other shows we have watched in common while continuing to observe our surroundings. "I must admit, though, that I did watch Emily in Paris right before we started this trip. Is that weird?" he questions. "God, no. That is a great show and they do a good job of showing Paris to the viewers. I would suggest also watching The Parisian Agency, which is a reality show about a realtor family in Paris. You will get France on a grander scale, outside of just Paris. Well, enough of that. We are in Paris. Let's get going. I suggest that we head to the Jardin des Tuileries, which is stunning, and then we can walk up the Avenue de L'Opera to see the Palais Garnier. After that, I am afraid we need to skip over to the Rue Saint Honore for some serious shopping," I respond. GG gives me the thumbs up, so we head out.

I try my best to narrate what I can remember of Paris as we walk the streets. He is so engaged and attentive, which is nice for a change. Then he gets personal. "So, Jane, you have been married before, is that right?" he asks. I tighten at the thought of Mark as he and I have walked these streets before. Sensing my shift, he puts his hand on my shoulder and says, "We don't have to talk about anything personal if you don't want to." "No, no, sorry, Dylan. It's fine. Yes, I was married, but my husband died early in our marriage. He was my college sweetheart. You know, you remind me a lot of him. He would be jealous right now," I say with a grin. "Jesus, sorry, Jane. I had no idea he had died. He must have been a great guy," he says as he nudges me, trying to take the seriousness out of the subject. We both chuckle and then walk on in silence. Not exactly awkward silence. More of a silence of understanding between two friends.

We tour the streets of Paris, keeping conversation light, then grab lunch at one of my favorite Parisian cafés', BREIZH Café Odeon. I am determined to eat as many crepes as I can handle.

After we both can eat no more, we hop in a cab to the Rue du Faubourg Saint-Honoré to pop into the major fashion houses. Serious shopping is not something I can do in pairs because it takes focus to spend a ridiculous amount of money. Kate gave me a spending allowance to spend on both of us since she really doesn't care about shopping. I am about to do some serious damage with this allowance, and I can't wait. Dior, Givenchy, Channel – oh my. My heart is pounding with excitement. It has been a while since I have done serious shopping like this. GG takes the hint and shares that he is going to grab a gelato just down the street but tells me to ring him when I am ready to head to the Rue Saint Honoré, which has lower-end, well-known brands. "Kate did say I needed to keep a watch on your spending, so shop wisely, Jane," he says with a wink. I give him a pouting look and roll my eyes as I turn on my heels and head for the Dior entrance. Fat chance.

It doesn't take me long to blow through the budget, but Kate is going to be tickled with what I picked up for her. We will have to drink champagne and do a "Sex in the City" closet fashion show when I get back. GG has been remarkably patient, and he managed to pick up a few things for himself along the way. After a good three hours of shopping, we decide to hail a cab and head back to the hotel for a cocktail before heading back to our rooms.

"I cannot wait to see how Kate got on with the executor. I am so curious about Kate's mother's uncle, which she knew nothing about. He seems so charming and is very involved with charities. Can't imagine why Kate's mother never spoke of him," I say as I plopped myself into a hotel lounge chair. I feel comfortable with GG now, and he seems trustworthy, so I continue by explaining why we are in Paris and on this 4-month trip as we sip on French martinis. Damn, these are good martinis, though I am starting to feel a bit weary from shopping and now two martinis. As we both sit, slumped in our oversized chairs, GG asks, "Don't you think it is about time you tell me what GG stands for? I mean, you really have me wondering, and I have come up with some possibilities that can be considered good or bad. Won't you put me out of my misery?" "Oh gosh, this is embarrassing. It's a college thing Kate and I used to do, and with her and I being together, just the two of us, I guess it has resurfaced. Okay. Now I am embarrassed because it was my idea to start this up again," I say. I can feel my temperature rising as my face flushes. GG isn't budging. He wants to know. "Fine. It stands for Greek God. There. I said it," I exclaim as I cross my arms, not looking Dylan's way. He bursts out laughing, then says, "Well, that is a relief. I won't tell you what I was thinking, but I'll take it because I do have Greek blood in me, and though I have never thought of myself as a God, I will take this as a compliment." I finally look over at him, and he is gleaming ear to ear with the sweetest smile. Geez…. he is a Greek God indeed.

Our slightly awkward moment is interrupted as Kate storms in with the biggest smile on her face, which turns into a puzzled look as she sees my red face and Dylan laughing. "There you are. Wait, what did I miss? Never mind. What a day I've had. I cannot wait to fill you in," Kate exclaims. Dylan, sensing we need some private time, stands up and thanks me for a fun and informative day. He leans down, takes my hand, and gently kisses it, which again makes me blush. As he walks away, he says, "Greek God out. Enjoy yourselves, ladies." The look on Kate's face is priceless. Our gig is up. She plops herself in Dylan's unoccupied seat and orders a martini as she turns her attention to me to begin. "Jane, you are going to have to fill me in later, but now, I need you to listen. This is all more than I had ever imagined, and I have a huge surprise for you that you are going to love. Do you need another drink before I get started?" she asks. As I am already quite buzzed, I shake my head no and lean forward to listen. Could this day get any better?

Chapter 29

Kate

My meeting with my great uncle's executor is at 10 am. I try to have one more conversation with my dad about this mysterious uncle, but the conversation was again fruitless. He just has no clue. Plus, his dementia is getting pretty bad. Tom was unable to uncover any further detail, so I am going into this quite blind but excited. As the driver expertly navigates the streets of Paris, I practice my introductions in French so that I can respectfully greet Delphine. She is a mademoiselle, so not married. Probably married to her work. My great uncle's office building is in La Defense, which apparently is a major business district just two miles from Paris' city limits. I like that they did not build this district in central Paris so that the city would not be obstructed by tall skyscrapers.

Within minutes, we arrive, and standing outside is a very posh petite woman, presumably Delphine. *Don't these French eat,* I think to myself. I guess when in fashion and cosmetics, one has to maintain a certain look. She waives, which confirms that she is indeed waiting for me. Delphine is stunning with her brassy golden hair and golden skin. She is wearing an emerald green silk blouse with a pencil skirt that has a slit all the way to the middle of her right thigh. Geez. That skirt is right up Jane's ally. As I step out of the car, she proceeds to kiss me once on each cheek, greeting me with "Bonjour, Kate! So wonderful to finally meet you!" I feel a bit unsteady, which she realizes, so she puts her arm around my waist to escort me into the building as she talks pleasantries. I don't even get to try my French out, as Delphine speaks perfect English. "I am so excited to be here in your lovely city, Delphine. I am anxious to learn about my mother's uncle, which sadly we know nothing about, but we feel that the connection must be Germany, where my mother's mother was from," I mutter with excitement. "Yes, exactly. I will tell you everything, but first, coffee? Espresso? Latte? What do you prefer?" Delphine kindly asks. "An espresso would be lovely, thank you," I quickly reply as we enter the all-glass skyscraper, which I learn is owned by my great uncle.

"I have an office for you to settle your things. Then, I will take you on a tour so that you can meet some of Monsieur Dubois' key business partners. They are anxious to meet you. There is Jean Marc, who heads up cosmetics, Camille, who heads up fashion, and Louise, who handles all of Monsieur Dubois' philanthropic activity. It was Monsieur Dubois' wish for the business to continue after his passing, so he set up the business as a partnership," Delphine explains. As we travel the executive suite hall, I stop in my tracks at a gigantic painting, presumably of my great uncle. The resemblance to my mother is uncanny. "Yes, that is your great uncle, Monsieur Dubois; God rest his soul. Doesn't he have the... how do you say...ah yes, kindest eyes? Kate, he was a remarkable man who was just as successful as generous. It must be a huge disappointment not to have known him and shocking for us to find that you were estranged. Well, we meet now. Voilà, ici," Delphine remarks as she ushers me into a beautiful office with French oak flooring and intricate crown molding. Though the office interior structure is French baroque, it is decorated very modern, which exudes artistic design. Jane would have loved this.

We chat as I sip on my espresso and take in my surroundings. Delphine lights up a cigarette and continues chatting, but I am distracted by her smoking. Ah yes. I am in Paris. Probably no restrictions on smoking here. Delphine describes my great uncle with such care and detail that the regret of not knowing him overcomes me. I lean further forward as Delphine begins to fill me in on what she knows from his childhood. Delphine relays that during World War II, my great uncle and his family were imprisoned in one of the concentration camps. As with most families, they were all separated, and as far as he knew, he was the only survivor. He made his way to France, once freed, and remained here ever since. Over the years he worked desperately to find his family while he poured himself into work. The war and separation from his family affected him terribly; he never married or had children. She explains very sadly that my great uncle, with the kind eyes, never quite got over losing his family. "Not until very recently did he have a lucky break from an American investigator. You see. He never gave up! Unfortunately, your mother, his sister's daughter, passed before he could reach her, but he was overjoyed to hear that she had a living daughter. You! Sadly, in the middle of planning a grand encounter with you, he passed, but not before he had already worked you into his Will. That was going to be his great surprise to you, Kate," Delphine exclaims with tears in her eyes. I didn't realize, but my eyes were welling up as well, and the tears began to stream down my face. Why did my mother not speak of him? Maybe she didn't know? Her mom had passed away a long time ago, so it may be that she did not want to speak of it – the tragedy, the hardship, the loss. I wish Tom was here to hear all of this first-hand. He is my rock, and right now, I need him. "I have more to tell you, mon cher. I have communicated to you the monetary inheritance which you now have, but there is more. Much more. Within the business partnership agreement, which I will share with you, it spells out that all of your great uncle's shares now belong to you, his only living heir, and you can either continue on as his legacy however you see fit, or you can sell your shares to the other partners," Delphine outlines. I must have turned white because Delphine stands up and rushes to my side, asking me if I am alright. I lean back in my chair, breathing slowly in and out until my dizziness subsides. Then, I stand up and begin to pace.

"Delphine, this is just too much to take in. He doesn't even know me. Why would he put this kind of faith in me? This is his life's work, and he wants me to be responsible for it, in part?" I exclaim. "Kate, please don't worry! This will not be a burden you will have to bear on your own. I am right here by your side to guide you through it all and his partners are long-time friends and colleagues that have his best interest at heart. We all will work through this at whatever pace or direction you wish. For now, just enjoy the moment of your good fortune, and once you are ready, let's go meet his part-ners. You will soon see that what your great uncle has built is extraordinary so you may find that you want to be a part of his legacy. That is our dearest hope, Kate, and was his," Delphine smiles broadly as she puts out her cigarette. The only thing I can think of is to hug her, forgetting that this is really not what the French do. Regardless, she takes my embrace and holds on until I decide to let go.

Once I recover, Delphine bounds into action to introduce me to the other partners. All equally handsome and beautiful. All equally kind and welcoming. Though I am impressed with what Jean Marc and Camille were responsible for, I am enthralled with Louise's overview of my great uncle's philanthropy. I am deeply moved to hear of my great uncle's hand in the Memorial De La Shoah. Louise explains that in Europe, nearly six million Jews were killed by Nazi Germany and its collaborators during the Second World War. Shoah is the Hebrew word for "catastrophe," which is different from what we in the US refer to as Holocaust. My great uncle apparently heavily funded the foundation and was the Board President. Louise brought a picture, which I soon learn is a picture of my grandmother, my great uncle, and their parents before being imprisoned. "Kate, I hope you have the opportunity to visit the Memorial during your stay, as you will see this same picture posted. You may have this picture to show your family if you would like," Louise states as he hands the picture over to me. As Louise proceeds to disclose the countless charities my great uncle supports, I can't peel my eyes away from the photo. Sensing that I am overwhelmed, Delphine suggests we go out for lunch and have a well-deserved glass of champagne that we will raise in his memory and in our coming together. I am already starting to adore these people. Not just because of how welcoming they have been. Their openness, honesty, and strong love and connection with my great uncle are amazing to witness and be a part of. I know that I want to be a part of this going forward. But how?

After an amazing lunch and several glasses of champagne, it is time to head back to the office. Before departing, Jean Marc reveals one more surprise to me, though much more for Jane, as this is right up her alley. Jane is going to lose her mind when I tell her. Several cheek kisses later, I am back in the office that Delphine set up for me. After Delphine departs, I close the door and walk over to the large desk. On the desk is a copy of the partnership agreement Delphine promised to share with me, along with several other documents, company annual reports, and key cards. I make a mental note to myself to have the receptionist email over the agreement to Mark, once I have a chance to speak to him. He's gonna shit. Oh, and Carly is going to go ballistic when she finds out about her now ties to the cosmetic and fashion industry. Jackson will love to hear about his great great uncle's patronage to the arts. All of this is just too good to be true and too much to handle on my own. It is too early to call Mark in L.A. so I will call him when I get back to the hotel after I debrief with Jane. After taking one more long look at what could be a very big part of my future, I rang the driver to let him know I was ready to head back to the hotel.

On the drive, I surmise that my grandmother must have changed her name upon arriving in America. After all, my great uncle had. I can't imagine having to push away your past and become someone else. It must have been scary and confusing. Delphine gave me the keys to my great uncle's Paris apartment, which will be maintained for my use whenever I am in Paris. Imagine. She said that all of his family documents are in his study, which I can go through at my leisure. I hope that Jane is up for going there with me as I don't think I can do that alone.

As I enter the hotel lobby, I spot Jane and Dylan sitting in oversized chairs, drinking cocktails. Jane is all red in the face and Dylan is laughing. Seems they must have had a good day, but what I have to tell her is so over the top that anything that has happened between them will have to wait. Dylan takes the clue and excuses himself as I sink into his chair, then order a drink and begin to recount everything that transpired. Jane's eyes begin to grow by the minute as she grabs my hand and holds it tightly. *Don't think I didn't notice those big shopping bags Jane,* I think to myself.

Chapter 30

Dylan

My long hair is getting harder to maintain, and my beard, which I don't usually have, is starting to annoy me. Even though Randy and Nathan don't know me, keeping my identity hidden is critical. I think I have convinced Randy that I am an average Joe with no agenda and really no ambition beyond travel and having fun. So much so that he slips a comment regarding a past colleague that he recently saw in Oahu. That doesn't bode well with his story that he only saw his family while there. Nathan is oblivious, as he often is, and takes no heed to Randy's earlier warning not to drink while on a job. "Hey Randy, when are we gonna introduce Dylan to the T-man, huh? He's cool. He's cool," Nathan blurts in a drunken slur. Rather than chastise him, in order to not bring light to what he just blurted out, I suppose, Randy quickly changes the subject, slipping a sideways glare at Nathan in the process. "So, Dylan, you seem to be getting to know our clients pretty well. Have they given you any indication as to when they want to leave for Greece? Paris is not my favorite," Randy says. "Nope, no clue. Mrs. Dunker seems to have some business here with the outcome unknown, so not sure what that means to the length of this leg," I reply. I give no indication that I noted Nathan's reference to the T-man, which presumably is Troy. Inside, though, my blood is boiling, as I am sure my ex-wife was with him in Oahu. Bitch. Randy rolls his eyes in frustration, then turns his attention to Nathan and says, "Jesus, Nathan, are you incapable of not over-doing your alcohol consumption? This is not going to bode well, if you know what I mean." Nathan scoffs at Randy and, in defiance, slams down his drink and stands up. "I think I've had enough of this. I am grabbing an Uber. Later," Nathan says as he stumbles off, using the furniture to keep him steady. *What a tool*, I think to myself. He is definitely going to be the kink in their grand scheme armor.

Randy pays the bill and leaves, clearly to go and deal with Nathan. I take the opportunity to call my father. He agrees with me that we are on the right track with our assumed connection between the three of them. He shares that a recent request came in from a wealthy Chinese heiress, requesting a private jet to fly her from L.A. to China and back. Coincidentally, Randy had called and asked to be switched to that flight with Nathan, making up some excuse as to why he needed to be in the US vs. being away for several months. My father explains that a wire transfer is pending but the heiress is insisting that the flight transpire immediately. Interesting that Randy did not give any indication of this in our earlier conversation. "We are pushing back, but son, I think this is one of Troy's setups. I can feel it," my father says. "Dad, I think you are right. I am doing some digging on Google right now on the heiress. I see her footprint but no real validation of her official heiress status, other than what they are saying on social media. Put Randy off, too. Looks like we will be in Paris for a while, and I am staying where Randy and Nathan are staying so I will keep closer tabs on their comings and goings. Don't worry. We have the right checks and balances in place now; there is no way they will be able to get away with another bogus transaction," I assure him. "Dad, one more thing. I took your advice and have also been enjoying myself and well, I have formed a connection with one of our clients. Keeping it professional, but I wanted you to know." I assure him that I am not going too fast and that I am doing my due diligence. It's amazing how a parent, with their line of questioning, can make you feel five again.

We hang up, and I hurry back to the hotel. My room is not anywhere near Nathan and Randy's, so I need to get moved so that I can see their comings and goings. Thankfully, there is a room right next to Randy's and across from Nathan's available so I take it and wait until well after midnight to move my things into the room. This hotel is several stars below where the ladies are staying, so the walls are paper-thin. I should be able to hear when they are moving and maybe even their conversations if I put a glass up to the wall. That makes me chuckle thinking of my childhood, performing this same act when I wanted to listen to what my sister and her friends were talking about when she had sleepovers. Doing it the old-school way as we are not sophisticated enough to tap rooms on this "undercover operation."

As I am just about to fall asleep, I hear a phone ring. It isn't mine, and it sounds like it is coming from Randy's room. I quickly jump up, grab the glass, and put my ear to the glass, then the wall. "Troy, what's the hold up with the heiress? Wait. What was that?" I hear Randy ask. Whoops. I shouldn't have slammed the cup against the wall. "Never mind, I thought I heard something. Anyway. I thought you had the method to prove funds down to address Jet World's updated verification process," he continues. Bingo. "Mr. Drakos is giving me push back on switching flights. We might have to bring Andy into this sooner than expected," he continues. Holy shit. This is it. "Are you sure this heiress has the necessary papers?" he asks. Then there is a pause, and he continues, "Fine, sounds good, Troy. Keep me posted. I also wanted to mention that we might need to cut Nathan loose as he is uncontrollable. The problem is I am not sure if we can keep him silent. It is going to cost us."

After a few more insignificant exchanges, I hear Randy hang up the phone, and then there is silence. I need to call my father immediately to brief him so that he can bring our lawyers up to speed, but I do not want to have this conversation in the room. I wait about half an hour, then head to the lobby. We have the connection. We know it is them. Now, how do we prove it? We might need to bring in professionals—the authorities. I don't think I am equipped to handle what needs to transpire next. My father agrees, which is a relief to me. I have done my part and have discovered what is happening. I am not going to get much sleep tonight, that is for sure. I can't wait to be able to tell all of this to Jane when the time is right. She already suspects there is some mystery to me. I hope I don't have to wait too long, which might put her off. Hell, she might not like me with short hair and no beard after this is all done. Nah, I personally think I look better that way. Gotta get some sleep.

Chapter 31

Jane

I feel like I'm in a dream, sitting on the edge of my chair, holding onto Kate's hand as she describes the events of her day. My mouth must have been open in disbelief the entire time because I was quite parched. I didn't interrupt her. I let her tell her story from beginning to end as I soaked it all in. When she seemed to be done, I waved the bartender over and ordered us martinis. Doubles this time around.

"Jane, say something? Anything? I am dying to hear what you think of all of this?" Kate exclaims in exasperation at my silence. I hold my hand up as if to say, let's just wait for the martinis, then I will talk. I need time to process. This isn't really even happening to me, so I can't imagine what Kate is going through.

When the martinis arrive, I take a large sip, place the glass down slowly and gently, grab my friend's hand again, and say, "I am just in disbelief, Kate. It was hard enough for us to comprehend the enormous inheritance, but this? A part of his large and successful business. His Paris apartment. It's life-changing, Kate! What are you going to do?" I ask. "I have no earthly idea, and I haven't even discussed this with Mark, but I feel a tremendous pull towards this opportunity that I cannot ignore. Of course, I have no experience with fashion or cosmetics, let alone philanthropy, but this isn't something that I can just give up and sell off to the partners when my great uncle has bestowed this upon me? Can I? Delphine said that it was his and their great wish that I join them in whatever capacity. I dunno, but I am exhausted, and my head hurts from all the excitement of the day," says Kate.

Then, the coup de grâce happens. From my perspective, that is. "Oh, and there's this. Now, this is going to make you scream, Jane, so try to contain yourself," Kate says with mischief in her eyes. "Jesus, what Kate? What could possibly top everything you have told me so far?" I exclaim. "Well, that certainly can't be topped from my perspective, but for you, my other news, well…. let me just tell you what it is. We. Are you ready? We are going to…. Paris Fashion Week," Kate shouts so loud that everyone in the lounge turns around. I slam my body back in my chair, put my hands over my mouth, and begin to squeal in excitement. Then I grab my friend, pull her up, and into a huge bear hug as we jump up and down in excitement together. I finally let go and we both slump back into our chairs and begin to laugh hysterically. "Try to contain yourself, Jane, because as part of this, Camille, who heads up fashion for Maison Dubois, told me we will be fashioned by none other than Dior! Yup, I said it. Dior. One of your favorites, right?" she asks, knowing damn well it's my favorite.

This was just too much to process. First, the news of her total inheritance. Then this! Attending one of the big four fashion shows has never been something I thought I would be able to do. I just don't travel in those circles. I simply like high-end fashion. Who would have thought that my friend, who snubs her nose at shopping, would be the one to get me to a fashion show? Let alone

Paris Fashion Week. "Camille has set an appointment for us at Dior for the day after tomorrow to be styled. In addition, she has scheduled us at the Dior Spa Cheval Blanc Paris for the works tomorrow to get us fashion-ready," Kate's eyes glisten with excitement as she details what she knows I would absolutely love.

Sensing her exhaustion and need to call Mark, I stand up, take her hand, lead her towards the lobby, and say, "Kate, you are a gift that just keeps on giving. Who would have thought two scholarship track runners from the University of Hawaii would be attending Paris Fashion Week? This is a dream come true for me for sure. You are just going to have to bear and grin through it," I say teasingly. "Your news just puts all that I bought to shame, but I hope you like what I picked up for you. I did purchase some Dior so we can wear those pieces when we go to the spa and to be fashioned out of respect to the brand." Kate nods and takes my lead as we walk through the hotel lobby to the elevators. "Why don't we go upstairs so that you can call Mark in private? Ring me when you are done. I think we should go for a swim to clear our minds. Then we can order room service and chill tonight. We can have our own mini fashion show with the stuff I got us! It has been quite a day for you. Does that sound good?" I say. She nods in exhaustion. Sweet Kate has quite a lot to process in the coming days and months. This might mean we cut our full travel plans short, but goodness, who cares? This trip has already exceeded my expectations with a bonus of Dylan, dare I say. With Kate's permission, I cannot wait to fill him in.

Chapter 32

Kate

The next several days were a whirlwind; I hardly had time to think about all that transpired with Delphine and the partners. Tom processed my new information with calmness and openness. He knew this gift horse was not something we could decide quickly, so we talked about going to Paris together once Jane and I finished our trip. We need to think about this, as a couple and family, to decide how we want to proceed. I was glad to accept any reprieve from having to deal with this on my own.

Carly threw a complete temper tantrum when I shared that we were going to Paris Fashion Week. I was only able to calm her down after explaining our new ties to the fashion and cosmetic industry, and of course, I hinted at bringing her something back from Dior, which rendered a squeal that almost took my eardrum out. How I would love to fly my whole family here to be a part of this now but I am going to honor my commitment to Jane and this trip, finishing what we started.

After our spa treatment at Dior Spa Cheval Blanc Paris, Jane took me to the recently renovated Galerie Dior for a quick history lesson on Christian Dior's House of Dior and how it changed the look of women's clothing forever. Despite my lack of interest in fashion, it was a beautiful experience seeing it with Jane. It brought what I have only seen in magazines to life. The grand staircase had a stunning presentation of Dior's items, but the most impressive and fascinating part of the gallery was the gowns, which were custom-made for some of the most important women of the 20th century. It was, simply put, a fairy tale, and we were living in it.

I am not sure I will ever be able to put into words to my family how incredible our day was experiencing Paris Fashion Week. I felt glamorous for the first time in my life, and I am not going to lie; I enjoyed it. Jane, of course, was in her element and had no trouble hob-nobbing with anyone Delphine and Camille introduced us to. I hadn't realized how much Jane actually knew about the fashion world until now. Thinking about it, I wondered why she didn't pursue fashion rather than medicine. Though she is an excellent nurse, she is abso-lutely glowing in this environment. This is a day neither of us will ever forget. Our day ended with a house party at Dior's Creative Director's home, Serge Ruffieux. At the house party, Camille shared that she sat on Dior's Board of Directors, hence the company's full participation in all things Dior.

Though exhausted from the prior day's event, Jane and I make a visit to my uncle's apartment, which is beyond gorgeous. I can totally see myself living here. I decide that now is not the time to start unraveling my family's past, but I will do that with Tom when we return. I take pictures of every room so that I can show my fam-ily as we contemplate our future ties to this city. Before leaving, I decide to call Delphine to let her know where my head is and what may be our next steps. "Delphine. Bonjour. Comment allez-vous?" I say as confidently as I can in a language I struggle to learn. "Kate! Très bien ma Chérie! Have you recovered? You and your friend Jane looked wonderful in your haute couture. Did you love what you were styled in?" Delphine responds in delight. "Oh, Delphine, it was more than we could have imagined. I don't think our feet have touched the ground since we were dressed yesterday morning. We cannot thank you and the team enough for the experience. I don't think we will be able to top that with anything we do going forward," I respond, equally delighted. "Je suis tellement contente Kate...very pleased that you enjoyed yourself. So, what is on your agenda in the coming days?" Delphine asks. "That's why I am calling you. I did speak with my husband, and like me, he is in shock, but it is a good shock. We would like to come back as a family after my trip is over so that we can focus properly on all that you put before me the other day. Would that be okay? We can stay at my uncle's apartment next time, which, by the way, is stunning. I know that you said everything is taken care of with the apartment but is there anything I need to be aware of or arrange for to ensure it is properly maintained?" I ask. "No, no. Everything is taken care of. There is nothing you need to do or worry about Kate. Sounds like an excellent idea for you to return with your family after your trip. You should just go and enjoy your time with your beautiful friend, Jane. All things are man aged here," she responds.

We need time. Tom is having our lawyers look over the paperwork Delphine gave to me, and he is doing research on his end into the company. By the time I get back from my trip, the kids will be out of school, so it will be a perfect time for us to travel back. Excited with the prospect of a future tie to Paris, I smile brightly as I hang up the phone and turn my attention to Jane. She was twirling around the apartment like a little kid on Christmas day. "Kate, I never want to leave here. Seriously! I could see MYSELF living here, honestly. You might just have to adopt me," she says with a wink. She is in her element. How great would it be for us to live in the city of Paris together? She would never leave her brother and her job. Surely not. "I know, right? I have to keep pinching myself to make sure this is real. I have touched base with Delphine so that is all settled. We should talk about our next leg. Jonathan plans to connect with us in Egypt, right? As a surprise, I am chartering another private jet to fly him to meet us. I have already reached out to Sasha to make the necessary arrangements, but she needs dates," I say, waiting for her reaction. "Kate, he's gonna shit himself! I want to be there when you tell him. That is so kind of you," she says as she gives me the biggest bear hug, which lifts me off of my feet. "Then it's settled, but first Greece. I cannot wait to immerse myself in Greek culture and eat feta with every meal. I say we head out as early as tomorrow morning, but first, Jane, I need to do some shopping of my own. I seem to have caught the fashion bug you have been plagued with all these years. You in?" I ask. "Seriously. Like you even have to ask. Yay! Let's go," she responds as she bounds to the front door. "I'll call Randy from the car to let them know so they can prepare. You must miss Dylan since you haven't seen him in a couple of days, aye Jane?" I ask innocently. She punches me really hard in the arm, which makes me cry out, and then we exit the apartment through the private elevator to the lobby, where our driver is waiting. This could be my life if I want. I think I definitely want.

Chapter 33

Jane

I'm in shock. Dylan is not who he posed to be, and we were all part of an ongoing investigation related to fraud within his father's company. When Kate attempted to call Randy, she couldn't reach him, so she called Dylan. Though not immediately available, Dylan called back and let us know that Randy would no longer be piloting our flight and Nathan has been pulled from the job as well. A new crew is on their way but will not arrive until the day after tomorrow, so we will have to delay our flight by one more day. He apologized profusely and asked if he could speak with us directly when we returned to the hotel.

Our minds are spinning, so rather than shop, we head straight back to the hotel and arrange for a private meeting space within the hotel where Dylan meets us. Dylan arrives in the room looking much different. His beard is gone, and his hair is short, revealing his even more beautiful face. I gasp but quickly compose myself as Dylan locks eyes with me. "Dylan? What the hell, Dylan? What is going on?" Kate asks quite anxiously. Dylan proceeds to tell us the full story, which explains why he is on our trip and why he appeared the way he originally did. I chuckle a bit on the inside at the possibility of being part of an undercover boss operation. Dylan's real name is Alex Drakos, which now fully explains the initials on his handkerchief. Apparently, a supposed heiress they were due to fly broke down in confession after being interrogated by the authorities, implicating all parties to the scheme, which included Nathan, Randy, and some ex-employee named Troy, which we learn is who his ex-wife cheated on him with, which led to his divorce. His divorce? Alex explains that during his time as steward, he uncovered evidence that supported their involvement, which he shared with his father, who took it to the authorities. This allowed authorities to act quickly, getting to the heiress first to render a confession. I am shocked to learn that he had been married before, but even more shocked at the idea that he is more than a steward. Though he owes his explanation to Kate, he looks at me mostly, trying to figure out what I am thinking. I sit in silence as Kate paces the room.

"This is really unacceptable, Dylan. I mean Alex. We could have been in danger, no? These are criminals. What if they caught wind of who you are and what you were doing and hijacked us?" she asks in astonishment. "Kate, I mean Mrs. Dunker. Please know that I completely removed myself as soon as I had the evidence I needed and I made very sure they were none the wiser. I would have done nothing to jeopardize your safety, nor would I have ever put you in any danger. These guys are criminals, but they are not violent. Just scammers. I assure you," Alex answers, a bit embarrassed at the oversight of possible danger to his clients. "Still, you don't really know what they are capable of. Do you? Jesus. So where are Randy and Nathan now?" Kate asks. "They were seized by the authorities about an hour ago and they will be transported to the US tomorrow. As I said, the new crew will arrive tomorrow, and we can leave for Greece the day after. We do apologize for any inconvenience this has caused you in delaying your desired departure time. You do understand that we did need to get this resolved so that it stops happening and doesn't run my father's company, my family business, into the ground," Alex responds, looking down at his feet.

With that, I jump in and say, "Kate, I don't think we were really in any danger, and I think we can bare one extra day in Paris, Oui?" I note as I grab my friend's hands and look into her eyes to reassure her. "I guess you are right, and you really couldn't have told us anything you suspected if you wanted to pull this off. I am intrigued but, at the same time, pissed. I'll get over it as long as we don't have any more of this on this trip. It's a done deal, right? Are all parties caught?" Kate emphatically expresses. "Yes, ma'am. All have been apprehended, even Troy and my ex-wife, who has been implicated in this," he says quite sadly. He has pulled on Kate's heartstrings, and I could see she is resolved. "OK, then that is behind us all. What are you going to do now, Alex? Are you leaving us?" Kate asks. "If you permit, I would like to finish the trip as your steward, of course. I would like to see this trip through to the end," he says as he glances my way. "Yes, of course. I am sure Jane would agree we wouldn't want to lose you as well," she states after looking at my pleading eyes. "Well, Jane and I have some shopping to do, but before we leave, I need to phone my husband and fill him in. I don't want him hearing this on the news. I am sure you and Jane have things to talk about. Let's connect in the lobby in an hour. Jane, does that work?" she asks. I nod, which she acknowledges, and then she leaves the room, leaving Alex and me in awkward silence.

Both Alex and I sit back in chairs in silence for several minutes before I break the ice. "Holy crap, Alex, I cannot believe you have been dealing with all of this. So much makes sense now that this has come to a head. You must have been freaking out?" I say in concern. Alex was grateful for the kindness and proceeded to tell me, from beginning to end, all that had transpired over the last year. Being deceived by your loved one like this is unimaginable, but he seems to have a loving and supportive family who all work together to get through this. He was thankful not to have had any children with her so that when he cut ties, he could cut them for good. Good riddance, I say.

As we are walking out to meet up with Kate, Alex grabs my hand and says, "Jane, I am really sorry, and I hope this doesn't disappoint you. I really have enjoyed our time, and I hope we can spend a little more time together, openly," he says. Was he blushing? "Honestly, Alex, this is more excitement than I have had in a long time. The outcome is surprising but in a good way. This is, quite frankly, a positive spin. Plus, you are dashing in your clean-shaven look," I respond, equally blushing when I spot Kate. Alex and I look at each other and bust out laughing as we approach her, and then he bids us goodbye as we head out to shop for the day.

After we settle in the car, Kate turns to me and says, "Well, that was an interesting spin, huh Jane? I mean, he's wealthy and more handsome than before. This might turn into a romance vs. a dalliance, I am thinking." "OK, Dear Abby. Calm yourself. I will admit I like Alex and have enjoyed my time with him. Let's just see what happens, K? You know he is Greek, right, and still has relatives in Greece, so he might prove useful on our next leg," I respond, trying to hide my surprising hope in what might be possible. "Useful indeed," Kate responds as she shifts to stare out the window. Geez, she is something else, this friend of mine. She made no further mention of the fraud.

We shopped until we literally dropped, then did it all over again the next day after we toured Versailles. We held a mini fashion show in Kate's room while drinking champagne, laughing so hard we peed ourselves. Kate is such a good friend. I recalled an old Irish proverb that says, "A good friend is like a four-leaf clover: hard to find and lucky to have." Kate is my four-leaf clover, which I will keep figuratively pressed in a book for safekeeping forever.

Chapter 34

Jonathan

Kate shared the unbelievable news. I am going to be flown to Egypt on a private jet! That almost makes up for not being fully part of this adventure my sister has been on for the last couple of months. I just cannot believe all that has transpired on their trip. Kate's new fortune. Paris Fashion Week. Their bout with crime. Jane's new romance.

They have been in Greece for a month, touring and soaking in the sun. Apparently, Jane's new beau is Greek, so they have had the real Greek experience. I would have met them in Greece if I hadn't already been there late last year. Plus, I don't think I would have wanted to watch my sister romancing with her new man. I loved Mark and miss him a lot. He was the adventurous one and always took me on any adventure he planned. I was grateful to have such a great brother-in-law. I miss him. I am not sure how this guy is going to measure up, but my sister sounds happy. She deserves it, as she has been wallowing in Mark's memory for far too long.

As I prepare for my departure to Egypt, I include plans to visit with one of our mother's uncles, who is still living in Alexandria, Egypt. He is 110 and still living independently. It'll be interesting to see how he gets on. I manage to squeeze in a dinner with him, in between the many activities Jane and Kate have planned.   The travel agent just sent me the itinerary, and it is jam-packed:

Dear Jonathan,

I am so excited for you to be joining your sister in Egypt. What a treat! The private jet has been secured with Jet World and is scheduled to depart on the 17th at 6 am. The flight will take approximately 10.5 hours. Kate requested a large jet so that your trip is non-stop. Please arrive at least half an hour before departure.

I have shared the below with your sister, which is the secured activity, as requested. This is sure to be a memorable trip. Safe travels, and don't hesitate to call me if you have any questions.

Activity while in Egypt:

Day 1 – Private Tour of Giza Pyramids, Sphinx, Memphis, Saqqara with lunch and camel rides (this was your sister's idea. I think she got it from the Sex in the City Movie 2 – LOL)

Day 2 – Egyptian Museum and Bazaar, then dinner with uncle

Day 3 – Private Tour Luxor, Valley of the Kings; Night cruise on the Nile

Day 4 – Sunrise Balloon ride

Day 5 – Overnight trip to Alexandria (dinner with great uncle)

Day 6 & 7 – Return to Cairo (two days un-planned, so relax!)

Day 8 – Return to Washington DC via Jet World

Hotel Bookings:

You have your own personal rooms at the following hotels, though they are adjoining to your sisters' rooms. Have fun with that! Don't worry. Her new beau is not staying with her. Wink Emoji.

*Cairo – **Four Seasons**, 35 Giza St, Oula, Giza District, Giza Governorate 12612*

*Alexandria – **Four Seasons**, 399 El-Gaish Rd, San Stefano, El Rami 1, Alexandria Gover-norate 5452053*

Best,
Sasha

I make a quick note to pick up my prescriptions and check in on Jane's house one more time before I depart. Her house was smelling a bit musty the last time I was there, so I better open the windows and air it out a bit. I have a gig at the Westover Market Beer Garden, so I'll just work from her house and go straight thereafter. The band is not too happy with me leaving with all the gigs we had lined up, but I secured them another bass player which they seem happy with. Like I would give up a free trip to play with those bozos. I think I have outlived my time with this band after 15 years. I really don't think that I will go back to playing with them when I return. I am tired of playing the same songs, gig after gig, with no new material in sight. Of course, I will give them some warning. Soon.

As I head out for a hike, I text Jane: "Sis, got the itinerary. Getting pumped. Big hug to Kate. Hope you are enjoying Naxos. See you in a couple of days. Love ya." Here comes the three dots as she responds. I must have waited two minutes, and then she responded, "XXOO – see ya soon, bro." Why in the hell did it take so long for her to type that? As if sensing my annoyance, she messages: "Sorry for the delay. Was drying off after swimming in front of the hotel. You were right about transparent turquoise waters. I want to move here! Thanks for the recommendation. Travel safe." OK. I will give her a break just this once. Time to hike Rock Creek and get my sweat on. I roll my eyes as I think what my sister would have said to that if said out loud. Gay. Yeah, well, I am, after all.

Chapter 35

Jane

Leg 4 - Greece

I miss my big brother, but I couldn't be more content sitting under a covered lounger on Plaka beach with Alex. Our relationship turned to romance quickly, and to put it mildly, I am head over heels. Kate has been so kind to allow Alex to share this experience with us as he has shared his beautiful homeland in return. We three get along famously, and Alex is careful to limit PDA in front of her, and I am careful to make sure my attention is on her when we are with her. There is no jealousy or insecurity. We all know how blessed we are.

Following a wonderful stay in Athens, where Alex introduced us to a family who we danced and ate with for five days straight, Kate had Sasha charter a private yacht so that we could move from island to island, on the Aegean and Mediterranean Sea, with ease. Such a different pace from our other destinations, which was a welcome change for all of us. We visited islands by day and by night while the yacht was cruising; we ate, drank, and played cards until we couldn't hold our heads up. All three of us were becoming quite tan from the sun, though Alex was this beautiful dark olive color, clearly due to his Greek heritage.

The boat came equipped with jet skis, which we used to get back and forth to each island and explore remote locations not accessible by land. Everything about Greece was as I remembered. So many beautiful scenic places and unspoiled beaches. The people were charming, and the food was divine. Kate insisted we eat feta cheese with every meal, so we did. We partied in Mykonos, hiked the trails in Crete, paddle boarded in Corfu while exploring the underwater caves and grottos, and Alex and I had a little romance in Santorini while Kate had a low-grade fever that kept her on board for 2 days. Once Kate felt better, we boated over to Milos to snorkel, then to Naxos, where we decided to dock for a few days and stay on Plaka beach at the Ammothines Cycladic Suites. My brother stayed there before and insisted it was a must-stay. He is exactly right. This is our last stop before heading back to Athens to catch our flight to Cairo. I think I could stay here forever. The hotel is owned by a husband and wife who provide heartwarming hospitality. Really, the entire staff is amazing. The hotel and grounds are luxurious but unpretentious. Modern but functional. Effortless minimalist purity was their aesthetic goal, and they nailed it.

"Jane. Alex. This has been the most remarkable leg of our trip, and that is saying a lot after Paris. Greece and its surrounding islands have so much to offer. I am so happy I came and I cannot wait to bring my family here. Jackson will for sure want to explore all of the historical sights and Tom will do any water sport available. My Carly will enjoy the endless shopping available on each island, I am sure. How about you, Jane? Would you come back?" Kate asks lazily. "I think a return to Greece is in my future," I say as I look over to Alex and wink. He returns the wink, which makes me smile. "I just texted my brother that I could move here. Right here on this island with these people. Maybe I will give up nursing and work at this hotel," I say jokingly. "Too remote for me. Plus, the idea of not being able to put my toilet paper in the toilet has me a bit grossed out," she scrunches her nose in response. Alex nods in agreement. "Yeah, not sure why the Greek sewage pipes are only two inches in diameter vs. the normal four inches that we have in the US," Alex responds as I look at him as if to say, how in the hell do you know that? "Well, that seems an easy fix to implement, which would make a world of difference to the experience in Greece," Kate responds, though as an engineer, she knows it's not an "easy" fix. I nod my head as I continue to gaze at the turquoise water. "Hey, should we have our last meal at the hotel, or should we head over to Nikos & Marias for some more pastitsio?" I ask. "Let's just grab a late lunch here and then head back to the port. I want to go back to that one shop with marble figurines. I would like to bring one back for Jackson. We can grab a drink in town before we head to the boat. Sound good?" she asks. We nod in agreement then all three of us settle back into our loungers before heading back to shower and change for our last meal on this beautiful island. I am going to miss this island, but most of all, I am going to miss the people of Greece. I have always felt so welcomed.

Chapter 36

Kate

Just as I planned, Jane and Alex are, dare I say, falling in love. My little fake fever seemed to have done the trick in Santorini. I was happy to give them a couple of days to really get to know each other. Plus, I wanted to spend a little time on my own reading through the mounds of paperwork Delphine had given me. Tom has been through the paperwork with our lawyers and everything is exactly how Delphine had explained. I am part owner of a large company in Paris. What in the hell am I going to do? I would have never imagined myself in this world, but here I am. Do I want to immerse myself in it? Could I give up engineering? Without a question, yes. I can't believe I am seriously contemplating this. But to what degree? Do I engage from California, or do we move to Paris? What about my dad? He is late in life and in a care facility with dementia. I couldn't take him with us. Or could I? So many questions that Tom and I mulled over throughout my two-day "fever."

I was also able to have proper catch-ups with the kids who are healthy and happy. Seems the cook and housekeeper I hired settled in nicely, and Jackson was enjoying them. Carly, not so much. The housekeeper is staying on top of her, making sure she doesn't try to slide out of the house with makeup. Good. Tom was relieved not to have to deal with it. Tom let the health caregiver go because Jackson was doing so well on his new medication, which was really controlling his asthma. Tom flew out to DC with Jackson to have a checkup with Dr. Shad, who confirmed that Jackson was doing remarkably well. This was such a relief to hear. If we do contemplate moving to Paris, we will have to make sure that we can continue to keep his asthma in check. Jackson was in sports again and was loving it. He proudly reported that Finley was his dog and slept with only him. I wonder if Finley senses that Jackson has something going on medically while the others don't. What a sweet dog he has blossomed into, and it looks like the housekeeper is keeping on top of haircuts. His coat was as white as snow, in direct contrast with his very dark nose. And balls.

As if no time had passed, Carly was still hung up on at least being allowed to wear lip gloss to school, claiming that she was in prison with her bags being checked every morning by the housekeeper. How dramatic. I calmly stated my position to her again, which I had done almost daily before I left — no lip gloss until 14 and no makeup until 16 (applied under supervision). I will not bend on this, nor will I bend on them getting a phone with the internet before they are 18. The negative influences on social media are immeasurable and it is not worth the risk. There are "light" versions of phones that I will consider at 14, as long as there is a need. I know that the position on the phone will be a difficult one to hold onto, especially with all the social pressures but it is for their own good. They'll understand. Someday,

Tom is going to need his R & R, which is currently scheduled to start two weeks after my return. He will only be gone for a week, which is what most of his friends could manage, and for Tom, it is enough. He was excited and grateful, to which my response was, what is mine is yours. He inquired about Jane and Alex and seemed convinced that Alex was a standup guy. He loves Jane like I do and only wants the best for her. I love that about him.

As I look at Jane now, she seems much like she was when she was with Mark. Happy. Calm. Secure. To think this new fortune of mine has brought her happiness again makes me smile as I soak in the last of our time in Greece. Greece, you have my heart. Until next time.

Chapter 37

Jane

Leg 5 - Egypt

Egypt is indescribable. I don't want to leave my great uncle after our visit as I am completely wrapped up in stories from my family's past. Plus, he is so adorable at 110. I am not sure if I want to live that long, but he seems to be happy and healthy. My very smart brother brings a small tape recorder along and tapes the entire conversation, with my great uncle's permission. Thank goodness he speaks English, albeit broken English. Though my grandmother and mother have described to us how they end up in Egypt, it is interesting to hear his perspective. Before we leave, he hands my brother and me two black velvet bags sealed with a string. As he hands them to us, he says, "Treasure these, but use them if you ever need to." The weight and sound it makes as he places them in our hands suggest coins, but out of respect, we do not look inside until we are back in our car and heading to the hotel. There are about 50 gold coins in each bag, meant for my mother but alas, she is no longer with us. It's a good thing we are flying private; otherwise, how would we get them out of the country?

Alex is taken by my great uncle, soaking in every word he utters. Asking question after question as if it will have meaning to him. I think his intrigue comes from

Egypt's connection to Greece. He shares that Alexander the Great, in 332 BC, invades Egypt with armies made up of Greeks and Macedonians. Apparently, Alexander the Great is welcomed by the Egyptians as they are ready to throw off the oppressive Persian control. Egyptian Greeks are called Egyptiotes, which simply means Greeks in Egypt. My uncle further explains that the first organized community is in Cairo back in 1856, and communities in Alexandria develop a few years after. One of the most interesting facts is that the first banks in Egypt are crafted by Greeks. Alex leans over and says to me, "Look, we even have history that connects us." A bit of a far reach, but I will take it. I squeeze his hand, which makes my uncle wink at me as if in approval. I look over at Jonathan, who doesn't seem as pleased. I can always tell when he has something to say, but it is not the right moment. He and I have not yet talked about Alex, so I am sure he has many questions. All in good time.

We return to the hotel, and my brother's desire to begin the inquisition begins. Kate, sensing this, bids everyone goodnight, as does Alex, as I silently tell him I need time with my brother. When they leave, Jonathan starts in. In a very sweet way, he starts with reminiscing about Mark, then he switches to worry as to how my relationship with Alex comes about. "I mean, sis, what do you really know about him? Is he all that? I mean, he lives clearly across the country. Are you planning on moving to California? I am super pissed he involves you and Kate in this fraud mess!" he exclaims. This is what I do. I let him get it all out. Knowing this, he takes a deep breath and says, "Let me get us a couple of drinks, then you can fill me in."

How am I going to tell my brother that despite me saying for so many years that I will never find a love like Mark, I think I have found love again? Jonathan has dealt with my endless ups and downs since Mark's death. I am sure his skepticism is high. So, I brace myself for his return. I calmly go through everything with him, starting with my sessions with Connie, the hospital's clinical psychologist. Meditation and yoga are step one. Stop wallowing is step two. Kate is really helping with step three, which is to open myself up to new relationships without comparing them to Mark. I explain that the attraction was there from the beginning, which makes him grimace. Details between siblings around sexual attraction never seem to move past uncomfortable for some reason. As I explain all to him, I start to question if maybe I am just caught up in all the mystery and excitement. My brother senses that I am questioning myself and says, "Look, sis, I am sincerely happy for you if you are really happy. Alex does seem like a stand-up guy, and you are not one to jump into things. I can see that this conversation is bringing doubt into your mind. Yes, I can read your mind, so don't question it. Since Mom and Dad are not around, I have to be the one to protect you. That's all. K?" I nod and the love I feel for my brother in that moment is overwhelming. Despite our differences (mostly political), we have always been close, which has made this life without my parents bearable.

We spend the balance of the next hour chatting about our family, our great uncle who was doing remarkably well for being 110 and our stashes of coins, which we examine in more detail. These little treasures must be worth a small fortune, and we know they were solid 18-karat gold. A quick Google check noted that an ounce of them will be worth somewhere around $2,000.00. I hand my stash to Jonathan and say, "You better hold onto these cuz you know I will misplace them. Just put them in your safe when you get home, please." He greedily takes them, pulls them both close to his chest, and whispers, "Mine!" Man child. Weary from our adventures, we decide to call it a night, and head to our rooms. As I look back at him entering his room, I make a mental note to thank Kate again for bringing my brother out here for part of this journey. Him being here makes it that much more special. I am one lucky woman.

Chapter 38

Alex

I can tell I am falling hard for Jane. Her family history is remarkable, much like mine. She runs as I do. She is as interested in experiences as I am. I can really see myself traveling the world with her. Plus, she is drop-dead gorgeous, and her smile makes me blush. We make, I'd say, a handsome couple. Having a relationship like this with this type of person really makes me wonder what I ever saw in my ex. My ex is nothing like me and now that I think about it, we rarely did things together because we really did not have that much in common. We got wrapped up in the L.A. hype, which is not me at all. Thank goodness I insisted on a prenup and made darn sure we did not have children at the onset. I knew something wasn't right, so my instinct was to watch and wait.

With Jane, I feel like I could go all in. No prenup. Children would be a definite yes. We do live pretty far apart, but I really can work from anywhere and with the support of my parents, I am sure I could tailor what I do to accommodate where I would want to live. The thought of progressing my relationship with Jane excites me. I think she feels the same. Maybe her brother will put her off me. Nah. Though protective, he seems like a reasonable guy, and he really loves his sister. Before he heads back, I will try to spend some 1:1 time with him to secure his good graces.

Things are back on track with my father's company now that the fraud has been dealt with. He knows I had it hard with my ex so he is being so supportive, letting me explore this relationship with Jane while acting as steward for the company. At least it justifies my pay.

As I am about to head to bed, there is a soft knock on my door. It is Jane. She fills me in on her conversation with her brother, which was a relief to hear. She lunges forward and plants a long kiss on me that knocks me a bit back. Easy Alex. It would be so natural to close the door and move the romance forward, but I do not want to do that. I kiss her back gently and then pull back while still embracing her. It is time for me to really confess my feelings. "You know I am head over heels, right? You are perfect and everything that I have dreamed of. I made a huge mistake with my first and learned from it, so I have gone into this relationship with my eyes wide open. I know that I want to be with you. Whatever it takes and whatever that looks like. Distance is just something to work through. I...," Jane pounces on me before I can finish my sentence, and as she covers my face in kisses, there are tears in her eyes as she replies, "I feel the same, Alex. I really never thought I would find love again, but here I am. I want to be with you, too; however, we can work it out. I can move anywhere and find a job as an RN. Heck, I could start a concierge service for nursing support and just do that from wherever. It will be important for us to be out of this fantasy world we have been living in and experience each other in real life, but I really have no doubts."

We embrace for what seems like a very long time before she lets go and steps back. There is nothing more to be said. We are both in, and that is all that matters.

After a final kiss goodbye, Jane leaves, and I sink back into my bed with a shit-eating grin that is starting to hurt my cheeks. It sure feels good to be happy again.

Chapter 39

Kate

I think we need to bring this party to an end. I am finding it harder and harder to concentrate on enjoying myself after learning about my full fortune in Paris. I ring Jane's room a couple of times to speak to her, but there is no answer. Her brother must be taking her through the wringer. I should leave it until tomorrow so I can sleep on it, anyway. As I am about to head to the bathroom to wash my face, there is a rapid, rather loud knock at my door, followed by, "Kate! Kate! Open up! It's Jane."

What I see in my dear friend's face is pure joy so her conversation with her brother goes well, or is there something else that happens? "Kate, I am on cloud nine. Are you tired? Can we order some room service? Maybe some champagne. I feel like celebrating. You are the best friend I could ever hope for. I love you dearly, you know," says Jane with glee in her voice but not making much sense. "I have so much to tell you, and I need you now," she continues with pleading eyes.

"I'm up for it. Just let me know what you want. I will order while you get changed. I want to talk with you too but I am going to wait until tomorrow," I respond. "Great. Hold that thought. I will be right back," says Jane as she disappears through the door. Before I can even hang the phone up with room service, Jane is back with the same smile on her face. I can only surmise that her conversation goes well with her brother and she has settled on moving forward with Alex.

"Well, Kate, you get your wish! I am in love, and I have you to thank for it. This trip. Meeting Alex. This fantasy is going to become a reality for me, Kate," she exclaims. She tells me everything from the beginning, ending with Alex and Jane confessing their love for each other. Now, I am smiling ear to ear, knowing that the heartache my friend has endured since the loss of Mark is finally coming to an end. To think that my fortune leads her to this is all the thanks I need. "We have no idea what our future will look like, how we will come together to really be together, but I am confident we will work it out. Oh, and Kate, I want to thank you from the bottom of my heart for bringing my brother out. Having him here has been so special," she says as she grabs my hand and kisses it.

"Girl, you know I would do anything for you. My heart is full hearing this from you. There must be some divine intervention for Alex to be on this exact charter, albeit a bit scary when we learn what is really transpiring. You both will work it out, but Jane, I have been thinking," I say with hesitation in my voice. I tell her my thoughts on ending the trip early to start to deal with what is placed at my feet. I apologize for any inconvenience to her and Alex but my heart is just not in it anymore. I need to be back with my family, exploring our possibilities. Just like a true friend, Jane's only concern is with me. "We have had a wonderful trip, Kate. More than either of us could imagine. I completely get what you are thinking and I think you are right. You need to begin to process this, and you need your level-headed Tom by your side to do that. I am ready when you are to head back. Don't give me and Alex another thought. What are you thinking? Head back directly from Alexandria? We don't have to go back to Cairo. I can handle the change in plans with Sasha if you would like. You tell me. I am on board with whatever you decide," Jane responds.

What a relief. I know she will understand though I think she might be a bit disappointed as she will have to separate from Alex for however long they decide. "Look, Morocco is on the way back, and I need to see where my beautiful friend is born. Do you think Jonathan can just join us on the return vs. flying back by himself? We haven't gotten the opportunity to really harass you yet! It really will only change his return by a couple of days, and we can drop him off on the way back to California," I respond, knowing good and well she will come back to California instead of going directly home. She nods and confirms Jonathan can swing it, so once the champagne and snacks arrive, we settle on the couches and talk. We talk about Ginny and her harrowing experience. We reminisce about the Paris Fashion Show and our beautiful gowns. We recant our favorite spots in Greece and admire how well Jane's great uncle is doing at 110—another beautiful memory in the books for the two of us. As the warmth of the champagne sets in, I nestle against my friend and fall asleep, as does Jane. The future is bright for us but for now, we are content, just being together.

Kate

It has been six months since our great adventure and our lives are about to change. Not just mine and my family's, but Jane's, too.

Within three months, Jane and Alex could not stand being apart, so they got married at the Ritz-Carlton at Lake Tahoe, and Jane moved to the West Coast. I was thankful to have my friend nearby, and rather than starting a new nursing gig, I convinced her to help me work through my future plans. Of course, I insisted on paying her.

I wasn't back more than a week before we made a family decision to uproot and move to Paris. I insisted on a quick family trip to Paris before we set it in stone, but that only solidified my family's desires. My husband and I gave our notice at our respective jobs and poured ourselves into planning our future with Jane's help. After months of discussion, it became clear that I wanted Jane by my side in Paris, helping me manage my part of the business. Her knowledge is invaluable, and I can really use her instinct and insight.

Jane had already realized where my head was going and confessed that she and Alex had already been contemplating what life in Paris would look like for them.

Alex has already been in discussions with his father about starting a private jet company hub in Paris. Shit, this is really happening.

Jane, Tom, and I made several trips to Paris to solidify our relationship with Delphine and the partners, and to confirm our shared intentions. They were overjoyed and couldn't wait for Jane and I to join them. Delphine helped me to secure staff to take care of my father upon arrival. I was not about to leave him behind. Tom is going to take some time off to get the kids settled in Paris before thinking about what he might want to do. He is already scoping out all of the surf spots in France, which can be found all over the country. He is excited about the prospect of experiencing surf on that side of the globe and I am more than happy for him to do so as he wishes. There is no coming down from this cloud 9 anytime soon.

Though we did not take our full four-month trip, what we gained from our experiences is immeasurable. Now Jane and I get to live our lives together. Working side by side. Raising our families together. Who knew that two young girls on scholarship to the University of Hawaii would end up running a company in Paris. Ginny knew. Jane and I took a quick trip to see Ginny, to check in on her and her husband's recovery. She proudly told us that she had no doubt in her mind that our friendship would last and that we would do great things. As soon as it was safe for both of them to fly, I vowed to fly them out to spend time with us in Paris.

As we board our jet headed to Paris, I look down at Finley, who is staring right back at me as I say, "Don't worry, buddy. You are coming with us. You better brush up on your French mon petit chien." I scoop him up and mount the stairs to begin our new life, as my great uncle would have wanted.

About the Author

Elizabeth Barnes is a debut American writer, who lives in Virginia Beach, Virginia. She was born and raised, mostly in Africa, due to her father's position as a U.S. Foreign Service Officer. She is married and has two children, both grown and on their own. Elizabeth has used her creative writing skills throughout her 30+ year career and dabbled in creative writing while in college. Her inspiration to write 5 Months and Counting came coincidentally but with the encouragement of friends and colleagues, she is debuting with plans to continue this writing journey.